Desperatio... ...r face rigid a... ...him, moving clo... ...ut climbed up her neck.

"I can't let you lie." He smiled. "Besides, you're no good at it. And the evidence will clear us."

Defiance shot from her glare. Her stubborn streak reared its head again. "You don't get to decide."

Her gaze was fiery hot. Her body vibrated with intensity as she stalked toward him.

He readied himself for the argument that was sure to come, but she pressed a kiss to his lips instead, shocking the hell out of him.

"There's been enough fighting for one day. I need something else from you."

He locked onto her gaze. "Are you sure this is a good idea?"

"No. Not at all. But I need to do it anyway."

RANCHER RESCUE

BARB HAN

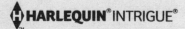
HARLEQUIN® INTRIGUE®

Recycling programs for this product may not exist in your area.

The chance to work with the incredibly talented Allison Lyons is a thrill beyond measure. Thank you for sharing your editing brilliance and giving me the chance to learn from you. To my agent, Jill Marsal, for all your guidance, encouragement, and patience.
To Jerrie Alexander, my brave friend and critique partner. To Brandon, who is strength personified; Jacob, who is the most courageous person I know; and Tori, who is brilliant and funny, I love you. This one is for you, Babe.

ISBN-13: 978-0-373-74798-6

RANCHER RESCUE

Printed in U.S.A.

www.Harlequin.com

CAST OF CHARACTERS

Katherine Harper—She is still reeling from her only sister's death when her nephew is kidnapped. When the kidnapper demands a file in exchange for her nephew's life, she has to race against the clock to figure out what this bad man thinks her secretive sister gave her before she died.

Caleb Snow—He's a North Texas horse rancher who, after a reckless youth, bought the TorJake Ranch to live a quiet life. When a stranger shows up on his land, he comes to her aid only to find himself embroiled in a kidnapping case and the target of a man who will stop at nothing to silence them both.

Noah—The four-year-old nephew of Katherine needs his asthma medicine to survive.

Matt—Foreman at TorJake Ranch, he always seems to be looking out for his boss's best interest.

Jimmy—His daughter is sick and he'll do anything to help her recover.

Kane—The powerful businessman, known to have politicians and police in his pocket, was linked to Katherine's sister romantically. Did she pay the ultimate price for leaving him?

Marshal Jones—He's assigned to the case, but can he be trusted?

Sheriff Coleman—He shares a mutual respect for Caleb. He'll stop at nothing, including arrest, to make sure Caleb is still walking the line.

ABOUT THE AUTHOR

Barb Han lives in North Texas with her very own hero-worthy husband, has three beautiful children, a spunky golden retriever/standard poodle mix and too many books in her to-read pile. In her downtime, she plays video games and spends much of her time on or around a basketball court. She's passionate about travel, and many of the places she visits end up in her books.

She loves interacting with readers and is grateful for their support. You can reach her at www.barbhan.com.

Books by Barb Han

HARLEQUIN INTRIGUE
1477—RANCHER RESCUE

Chapter One

Katherine Harper pushed up on all fours and spit dirt. "Don't take him. I'll do whatever you say."

The tangle of barbed wire squeezed around her calf. Pain scared her leg.

"She got herself caught." The man glared down at her. He glanced toward the thicket, sized up the situation and turned to his partner. "She's not going anywhere."

The first man whirled around. His lip curled. Hate filled his eyes. "Leave her. We have the boy."

"Kane won't like it. He wants them both."

"No. Please. My nephew has nothing to do with any of this." She kicked. Burning, throbbing flames scorched her ankle to her thigh. "I'll give you whatever you want. I'll find the file."

"We know you will. Involve the police and he's dead," the second man warned. "We'll be in touch."

Noah screamed for her. She heard the terror in his voice. A wave of hopelessness crashed through her as she struggled against the barbs, watching the men disappear into the woods with her nephew. *Oh. God. No.*

"He's sick. He needs medicine," she screamed through burning lungs.

They disappeared without looking back.

Shards of pain shot up her leg. Fear seized her. The thick trees closed in on her. Noah had been kidnapped, and she was trapped and helpless.

"Please. Somebody."

The thunder of hooves roared from somewhere in the distance. She sucked in a quick breath and scanned the area. Were more men out there?

Everything had happened so fast. How long had they been dragging her? How far into the woods was she?

All visual reminders of the pumpkin patch were long gone. No open fields or bales of hay. No bursts of orange dotting the landscape. No smells of animal fur and warmth. There was nothing familiar in her surroundings now.

Judging from the amount of blood and the relentless razor-sharp barbs digging into her flesh, she would bleed to death.

No. She wouldn't die. Noah needed her to stay alive. *Noah.*

Anger boiled inside her, heating her skin to flames. Katherine had to save him. He had no one else. He was probably terrified, which could bring on an asthma attack. Without his inhaler or medication, the episode could be fatal.

Forcing herself to her feet, she balanced on her good side and hopped. Her foot was slick with blood. Her shoe squished. Her knees buckled. The cold, hard ground punished her shoulder on impact.

She scrambled on all fours and tried to crawl. The barbed wire tightened like a coil. The ache in her leg was nothing compared to the agony in her heart.

Exertion wasn't good. Could she unwrap the mangled wire? Could she free herself? Could she catch up?

Panic pounded her chest. Her heartbeat echoed in her ears.

The hooves came closer. Had the men sent company? Had her screaming backfired, pinpointing her location?

Autumn foliage blanketed the ground, making it difficult to see if there was anything useful to use against another attacker. She could hide. But where?

The sounds of hooves pounding the unforgiving earth slowed. Near. She swallowed a sob. He could do whatever he wanted to her while she was trapped. Why had she made all that noise?

She fanned her hands across the ground. Was there anything she could use as a weapon? The best one encased her leg, causing a slow bleed. She needed to think. Come up with a plan. Could she use a sharp branch?

Biting back the pain, she scooted behind a tree and palmed a splintered stick.

The thunderous drumming came to a stop. The horse's labored breath broke through the quiet.

An imposing figure dismounted, muttering a curse. His low rumble of a voice sent chills up her neck.

Her pulse raced.

His boots firmly planted on the ground, Katherine got a good look at him. He was nothing like her attackers. They'd worn dark suits and sunglasses when they'd ambushed her and Noah. Everything about this man was different.

He wore jeans, a button-down shirt and a black cowboy hat. He had broad shoulders and lean hips. At his full height, he had to be at least six foot two, maybe more.

A man who looked genuine and strong like him couldn't be there for the wrong reasons, could he? Still, who could she trust? Couldn't murderers be magnetic?

"What in hell is going on?" A shiver raced up

her spine as he followed the line of blood that would lead him right to her.

He took a menacing step toward her. Friend or enemy, she was about to come face-to-face with him.

Katherine said a silent protection prayer.

Her equilibrium was off. Her head light. She closed her fingers around the tree trunk tighter. Could she hold on long enough to make her move?

A dimpled chin on a carved-from-granite face leaned toward her. Brown eyes stared at her. She faltered.

Nope. Not a hallucination. This cowboy was real, and she was getting weak. Her vision blurred. She had to act fast.

With a final push, Katherine stepped forward. Her knees buckled and she stumbled.

IN ONE QUICK motion Caleb Snow seized the stick being jabbed at his ribs and pinned the woman to the ground.

She was gorgeous in her lacy white shirt. Her sea-green skirt hiked up her thigh far enough to reveal a peek of her panties. Pale blue. He swallowed hard. Tried not to think about his favorite color caressing her sweet little bottom as he wrestled to keep her from stabbing him. The rest of her was golden skin and long legs. She had just enough curves to make her feel like a real woman, sensual and soft. "What's wrong with you?"

The tangle of chestnut hair and limbs didn't speak.

Was she afraid? Of him? Hell no. He took the stick and tossed it. She kicked and punched.

"Hold still. I'm trying to help."

"No. You're not."

"I will as soon as I'm sure you won't try to poke me with that stick."

He'd turned his horse the moment he'd heard the screams that sounded half wild banshee, half horror-film victim expecting to help, not be attacked.

"You're hurting me," she yelped.

The tremor in her voice sliced through his frustration. Her admission tore through him. The thought he added to her pain hit him hard. "Stop trying to slap me, and I'll get up."

Her lips trembled. She looked at him—all big fearful eyes and cherry lips—and his heart squeezed.

Those violet eyes stared up at him, sending a painful recollection splintering through his chest. She had the same look of terror his mother always had right before his father'd raised a hand to her. Caleb buried the memory before it could take hold.

"Listen to me. I'm not going to hurt you." Her almond-shaped face, olive skin and soft features stirred an inappropriate sexual reaction. Skin-to-skin contact was a bad idea. He shifted more of his weight onto his bent knee.

Her breaths came out in short gasps. "Then let me go. I have to find him before they get away."

"As soon as I know you're not gonna do something stupid, I will. You're not going anywhere until I get this off your leg. You want to tell me what the hell's going on? Who's getting away?" Her actions were that of a wounded animal, not a crazed murderer. He eased more weight off her, scanning her for other injuries.

She recoiled. "Who are you?"

"Caleb Snow and this is my ranch." He picked up the wire to untangle her. Her pained cry pierced right through him. "Sorry about that." He eased the cable down carefully. "Didn't mean to hurt you."

She'd seriously tangled her long, silky leg in barbed wire. She'd lost a lot of blood. He couldn't have her going into shock. "The more you fight, the worse it'll get. You've done a number on yourself already."

Her eyelids fluttered.

Based on her pallor, she could lose consciousness if she didn't hold still. He stood and muttered a curse.

Her wild eyes looked up at him, pleading. "Some men took my nephew. I don't know who. They went that way." She motioned toward the

McGrath ranch. Her voice cracked and he could see she was struggling not to cry. Tears fell anyway.

"The wire has to come off first. Then we'll take a look. Don't watch me. It'll only hurt worse. Tell me your name." A stab of guilt pierced him at the pain he was about to cause. The weight of her body had impaled the rusty steel barbs deep into her flesh.

Her head tilted back as she winced. She gasped but didn't scream, her eyes still radiating distrust.

"Hold on. I have something that can help." He pulled wire cutters and antibiotic wipes from his saddlebag. He tied a handkerchief below her knee to stem the bleeding.

"Promise you won't leave me here?"

"Now why would I do that?" One by one, he pulled the barbs out of her skin, giving her time to breathe in between. "Tell me more about the men."

"They. Were. Big." The words came through quick bursts of breath.

He pulled the last barb and stuck his hand out, offering a help up.

Hers felt soft and small. A jolt of electricity shot up Caleb's arm. Normally he'd enjoy feeling a sexual spark. This wasn't the time or place.

"I need to go that way." She pointed north, grasping at the tree.

"You're hurt. On my property, that means you

don't go anywhere until I know you're okay. Besides, you still haven't told me why you're out here to begin with."

"Where is here?" she asked, dodging his question.

"The TorJake Ranch." How did she not know where she was? A dozen scenarios came to mind. None he liked. He took a step toward her. She was too weak to put up a fight. He wrapped his arm around her waist for support. "You aren't going anywhere like this. Start talking and I might be able to help. I have medical supplies at the house. But you'll explain why you're on my land or I'll call the sheriff. We clear?"

"Please. Don't. I'll tell you everything." He'd struck a nerve.

He should call Sheriff Coleman. No good ever came from a woman caught in a situation like this. But something about her made Caleb wait.

"My name is Katherine Harper. I took my nephew to a pumpkin patch." She glanced around. "I'm not sure which way."

"The Reynolds' place." Was it the fear in her eyes, or the tremble to her lips that hit him somewhere deep? He didn't care. He was intrigued.

"Sounds right. Anyway, two men in suits came from nowhere and grabbed us. They dragged us through the woods…here…until I got caught up. Then…"

Tears streaked her cheeks. "They took off with him."

The barbed wire had been cut. The McGrath ranch was on the other side of the fence. He'd have to ask about that. Of course, he preferred to deal with creatures of the four-legged variety or something with a motor.

"We'll figure this out."

Caleb assessed her carefully.

Her vulnerable state had his instincts sounding alarm bells.

Chapter Two

Noah was gone. Katherine was hurt. Her only chance to see her nephew again stood next to her. The cowboy's actions showed he wanted to help. He needed to know the truth. She couldn't pinpoint the other reason she felt an undeniable urge to confide in the cowboy. But she did.

"My nephew was kidnapped for a reason." *Oh. God.* It was almost unbearable to say those words out loud.

His thick brow arched. "Do you know these men?"

She shook her head. "They wanted me to give them a file. Said they knew I had it, but I don't. I have no idea what they're talking about."

The cowboy's comforting arm tightened around her. Could he really help? Noah was gone and she was desperate.

He pulled out his cell phone.

"I'm calling my foreman, then the sheriff. We'll cover more ground that way."

"No police. They insisted. Besides, there's no time. Let's use your horse. We might be able to catch them. Noah needs medicine." She moved to step forward. Pain nearly buckled her knees. Her vision blurred.

"Hold on there," he said, righting her again with a firm hand. "We'll find him, but I'm bringing in the law."

"They'll hurt—"

"I doubt it. Think about it. They'd say anything to back you off. There's no chance to find him otherwise." He turned to his call. "Matt, grab a few men and some horses. We have a situation. A boy's been taken. Looks like they might've crossed over to the McGrath place with him. I want every square inch of both properties scoured. And call the sheriff." His gaze met Katherine's, and her heart clutched. He was right. They were most likely bluffing.

She nodded.

"There are two men dressed in suits. Could be dangerous." His attention shifted to her. "How old is your nephew?"

"Four." With reinforcements on the way, she dared to think she could get Noah back safely before the sun went down.

A muscle in the cowboy's jaw ticked. "You heard that, right?" A beat later came, "Somebody cut the fence on the north corner. Jimmy's been running this side. Ask him how things were the other day when he came this way."

Katherine looked at the barbed wire. The last bit of hope this could have been a bad dream shriveled and died.

"Tell the men to be careful." Caleb took more of her weight as he pocketed his phone. "I've got you."

"I'm fine." Katherine struggled to break free from his grip. Her brain was scrambled. She'd been dragged through this area thinking it had been a random trail, but how could it be? They'd cut the fence in advance. Everything about them seemed professional and planned. But what kind of file could she possibly have for men like them?

The cowboy's strong grip tightened around her as she fought another wave of nausea. "I think I'll be fine once I get on your horse."

"My men are all over this. Matt's phoning the sheriff as we speak. I need to get you home where I can take care of your injuries. The sheriff will need to speak to you for his report."

"The longer I wait, the farther away Noah will be." She had no purse, no ID and no money. Those had been discarded along with his medicine. Everything she'd had with her was scattered between here and the pumpkin patch.

His brow arched. "You won't make it a mile in your condition."

"I can. I have to." Katherine tried to put weight on her foot. Her knee buckled. He pulled her upright again with strong arms. He was powerful, male and looked as though he could handle himself against just about any threat.

Caleb shook his head. "Hell, I'd move heaven and earth if I were in your situation. But you're hurt."

"He needs me. He's little and scared. You can't possibly understand." Her voice hitched.

The lines in the cowboy's forehead deepened. "We'll cut through the McGraths' on the way to the house. How's that?"

His arms banded around her hips. Arms like his would be capable of handling anyone or anything they came across. He lifted her onto the saddle with no effort and then swung up behind her.

"I need to make sure you're going to be around long enough to greet him. You let infection set in and that leg will be no use to you anymore."

She didn't argue. Fatigue weighted her limbs, drained her energy. If he could fix her leg, she could find Noah.

Taking the long way around didn't unearth any clues about Noah's whereabouts. The sky was darkening. Night would fall soon.

The house coming into view was a white two-story Colonial with a wraparound porch and dark green shutters. An impressive set of barns sat behind the house. There was a detached garage with a basketball hoop off to the side. This was a great place for kids.

Katherine hadn't stopped once to realize this man probably had a family of his own. The image of him cradling a baby edged its way into her thoughts. The contrast between something so tiny and vulnerable against his bare steel chest brought shivers up her arms.

Did he have a son? His reaction to Noah's age made more sense.

She prayed Noah would be home in bed before the sun vanished. Was he still panicked? Could he breathe? Did he have time before the next attack? Did she?

What would happen when the men came after her again if she couldn't produce the file?

She shrugged off the ice trickling down her spine. Police would need a description of the attackers. She had to think. The last thing she remembered was being hauled through the woods. She ran so long her lungs burned. The next thing she knew, she was facedown in the dirt. The men had disappeared. She'd lost everything.

"Lean toward me. I'll catch you." Caleb stood next to the horse.

One of his calloused but gentle hands splayed on the small of her back. He carried her inside as if she weighed nothing and placed her on the sofa in the front room. He lifted her bloody leg to rest on top of the polished knotty-pine coffee table.

The smell of spices and food warming sent a rumble through her stomach. How long had she been dragged? She wouldn't be able to eat, but how long could Noah go without food? Was he hungry?

"Margaret, grab my emergency bag," Caleb shouted before turning to Katherine. "Margaret helps me out with cleaning and cooking. Keeps me and my boys fed."

So he did have children. Katherine figured a place with this kind of space had to have little ones running around. Noah would have loved it here.

A round woman padded into the room. A salt-of-the-earth type with a kind face, she looked to be in her late fifties. Her expression dropped. "What happened?"

Caleb gave her a quick rundown before introducing them. "I'll need clean towels, a bowl of warm water and something for Katherine to drink. Some of these gashes are deep."

Margaret returned with supplies. "If anyone can find your nephew, it's this man."

Margaret's sympathetic expression melted some of Katherine's resolve. "Thank you."

"You look like you're in pain. Tell me where it hurts."

"My head. Stomach." Her hand pressed against

her midsection to stave off another round of nausea. "But I'll be fine."

"Of course you will. You're in good hands." She set a cup of tea next to Katherine. "This'll help."

She thanked the housekeeper, smiled and took a sip. "Tastes good."

"Would you mind grabbing the keys to my truck? Call the barn, too. I rode Dawn again. Ask Teddy to put her up for the night." Caleb patted one of Katherine's gashes with antibiotic ointment.

She gasped, biting back a scream. "Now that I'm okay, we're going to find them ourselves, right?"

"I'm taking you to the E.R."

"No." Shaking her head made everything hurt that much worse. "I can't leave. Your guys will find Noah and bring him here, right?"

"Yes."

"Then the only reason I'd walk out that door is to help search for him. I won't leave here without him. He needs me and his meds."

She expected a fight but got a nod of agreement instead.

Caleb went back to work carefully blotting each gash without saying another word. Trying to distract herself from the pain, Katherine studied the room. The decor was simple. Substantial, hand-carved wood furniture surrounded the fireplace, which had a rust-colored star above the mantel.

The cushions were soft. The place was more masculine than she figured it would be. There had to be a woman somewhere in the picture. A protective, gorgeous man like Caleb had to have a beautiful wife. And kids. She'd already envisioned him holding his child. She could easily see him with two or three more.

There was one problem. Nothing was out of place. She knew from spending the past week with Noah, kids left messes everywhere. "I hope your wife doesn't get the wrong impression when she sees a strange woman on your sofa."

Caleb didn't look up. "I'm single."

Had she met him under other circumstances, the admission would've caused a thousand tiny butterflies to flutter in her stomach. But now she could only think about Noah.

"Do you want to call Noah's parents and let them know what's going down?"

"No. There's no one else. His mother died. I'm all he's got." *The poor kid.*

Her sister, Leann, had always been the reckless one. Everything had been fun and games and risk for her. Now she was gone and Noah was in trouble.

A hundred questions danced across Caleb's intense brown eyes. To his credit, he didn't ask any of them.

Katherine figured he deserved to know the

truth. "She died in a climbing accident at Enchanted Rock a week ago. She was 'bouldering,' which apparently means you don't use safety equipment. You're supposed to have people spot you, but she didn't."

Caleb's jaw did that tick thing again. She'd seen it before when he'd seemed upset and held his tongue. Did he have something he wanted to say now?

"Sorry for your loss. This must be devastating for you. What about Noah's father?"

"She...the two of them...lived in Austin alone. She never told me who his father was. As far as I know, no one else has a clue, either. My sister may have been reckless with her actions but she could keep a secret." Katherine wondered what else she didn't know about Leann.

"Be easy enough to check out the birth certificate."

A half-laughed, half-exacerbated sigh slipped out. "She put down George Clooney."

If Caleb thought it funny, he didn't laugh.

Katherine cleared her throat. "I doubt if the father knows about Noah. Leann never told anyone who she dated. Not even me. I never knew the names of her boyfriends. When she spoke about them, they all had movie-star nicknames."

"There must've been a pattern to it."

Katherine shrugged. "Never gave it much thought before. Figured it was just for fun."

His reassuring nod comforted her.

"You two were close?"

"Our relationship was complicated, but I'm… was…fiercely protective of her." Katherine squeezed her elbows, not wanting to say what she really feared. Her sister had shucked responsibility and become involved with something or someone bad, and now both Katherine and Noah were in danger. Things had been turning around for Leann. Why would she do it?

Katherine tamped down the panic rising in her chest.

No one could hurt Noah.

She had to believe he would come home safely. Even though every fiber in her being feared he was already panicked, struggling to breathe. What if she found him and couldn't help? Her purse was lost along with his medicine.

One of Caleb's eyebrows lifted. "What about her friends?"

"I don't have the first idea who they were. My sister was a free spirit. She moved around a lot. Took odd jobs. I don't know much about her life before Noah. It wasn't until recently she contacted me at all." Had Leann known something was about to happen? Was she connected to the file?

Caleb didn't look at her. He just went back to work on her leg, cleaning blood and blotting on ointment.

Oh, God. Bile rose in her throat. Acid burned a trail to her mouth. "No news is definitely not good news."

"There aren't a lot of places to hide. If your nephew's around here, we'll find him. My men know this property better than they know their own mothers."

His comfort was hollow. A wave of desperation washed through her. If the men got off the property with Noah, how would she ever locate him?

"You hungry?"

"You know, I'm starting to feel much better." She tried to push up, but her arms gave out.

"Eat. Rest. The pain in your leg is only beginning. You must've twisted your ankle when you fell. It's swelling. Stay here. Keep it elevated. I'll check in with my men."

Caleb disappeared down the hall, returning a moment later with a steaming bowl in one hand and a bag of ice in the other. He'd removed his cowboy hat, revealing sandy-blond hair that was cut tight but long and loose enough to curl at the ends.

He set down the bowl before placing a pillow behind her head and ice on her ankle. He pulled out his cell while she ate the vegetable soup Margaret had prepared.

There was a knock at the front door. Katherine gasped. Her pulse raced.

CALEB'S EYES MET Katherine's and the power of that one look shot straight to his core. Her on his couch, helpless, with those big eyes—a shade of violet that bordered on purple in this light—made him wish he could erase her pain.

He let Sheriff Coleman in. The officer's tense expression reflected Caleb's emotions. "Your coming by on short notice is much appreciated."

Coleman tipped his hat, a nod to the mutual respect they'd built for one another in the years Caleb had owned the ranch.

"My men are out looking as we speak. I'll need more details to file the report."

Caleb introduced Coleman to Katherine. "This is the boy's aunt. He was with her at the Reynolds' pumpkin patch when it happened."

Sheriff Coleman tilted his head toward Katherine. His lips formed a grim line. "Start from the beginning and tell me everything you remember."

She talked about the pumpkin patch.

"Do you have a picture we can work with?" he asked, looking up from his notepad.

Her head shook, her lips trembled, but she didn't cry. "No. I don't. Lost them along with my purse and everything else I had with me. Not that it would do any good. He's only been living with me for a week. We haven't been down to clean his mother's apartment yet. I don't have many of his things. A few toys. His favorite stuffed animal."

She rambled a little. Not many women could hold it together under this much duress. Her strength radiated a flicker of light in the darkest shadows of Caleb. Places buried long ago, which were best left alone.

"Let's go over the description then," Coleman suggested.

"Black hair. Big brown eyes. Three and a half feet tall. About forty pounds. He's beautiful. Round face. Full cheeks. Curly hair. Features of an angel."

"And the men who took him?" he pressed.

"One of them had gray eyes and a jagged scar from the left side of his lip. He had a dark tan."

"How big was the scar?"

"Not more than a couple of inches. It was in the shape of a crescent moon." She sobbed, but quickly straightened her shoulders and shook it off.

The sheriff glanced away, giving her a moment of space. Caleb dropped his gaze to the floor, respecting her tenacity even more.

"He mentioned the name Kane. He said 'Kane wouldn't like it.'"

"We'll run the name against the database."

"I'm sorry. It's not much to go on. My nephew is alone. Sick. Scared. If he gets too upset, he could have an attack. Without his inhaler or medication, he won't be able to breathe."

Silence sat in the air for a beat.

Coleman cleared his throat. If Caleb didn't know any better, he'd say the sheriff had moisture in his eyes. In this small town, they didn't deal with a lot of violent crime.

"We'll do everything we can to bring him back to you safe and sound. That's a promise," Coleman said.

"Thank you."

"What's Noah's last name?"

"Foster."

"You said you haven't had a chance to clean out his mother's place. Where's that?"

"Austin."

"That where you're from?"

She shook her head. "I live in Dallas."

Caleb could've told the sheriff that. She had a polished, city look. The jeweled sandals on her feet were one of the most impractical shoes she could wear to the country aside from spiked heels.

"When's his birthday?"

"March. The seventeenth."

Caleb looked at her. He could see the tension in her face muscles and the stress threatening to crack, but to her credit, she kept her composure. Probably needed to be strong more than she needed air. Caleb knew the feeling for reasons he didn't want to talk about, either.

He'd known she was different from any other woman he'd met when he'd showed up to help her and she'd thanked him with a makeshift knife to his ribs. Hell, he respected her for it now that he knew the circumstances. She'd probably believed he was working with whoever had taken Noah and that he'd showed up to finish the job. She'd bucked up for a fight.

When she pushed herself up, it took everything in him not to close the distance between them and pull her into his arms for comfort. No one should have to go through this alone.

If Katherine Harper wanted to do this her way, he wouldn't block her path.

The sheriff asked a few more routine-sounding questions, listening intently to her answers. "You fight with anyone lately? A boyfriend?"

Caleb tried not to look as though he cared about the answer to that question. He had no right to care.

Katherine looked down. "Nope. No boyfriend."

"What about other family?"

"None. My parents died during my freshman year of college."

He didn't want to think about what that would do to a person.

Coleman asked a few more questions about family. Katherine looked uncomfortable answering.

"I'll notify my men to keep an eye out for your belongings. What were you doing out here with your nephew?"

"I wanted to take his mind off things. Get him out of the city. We planned our trip all day yesterday. He'd never seen a pumpkin patch. He loved the open space. I didn't think much about letting him run around. We've been in my small apartment all week. Didn't look to be anything or anyone else around for miles. He followed a duck out to the tree line. When I went over to take pictures, two men came from nowhere and snatched us. I panicked. Couldn't believe what was happening. I remember thinking, 'This can't be.' I fought back. That's when I ended up tangled in the barbed wire and they took off. If only I hadn't been so stubborn. If I hadn't fought."

"Don't blame yourself for this," Coleman said quickly.

"They told me if I came any closer or called the police, they'd kill him."

The sheriff nodded, but Caleb caught a flash behind Coleman's eyes. Caleb made a mental note to ask about that when they were alone.

"Ever see them before or hear their voices?"

Coleman's gaze was trained on his notepad as he scribbled.

"No. Nothing about them was familiar. They asked for a file, but I don't have the first clue what they were talking about. Wondered if they'd confused us with someone else."

Katherine continued, "I don't remember tossing my purse or jacket, but I must've ditched them both somewhere along the way. Noah needs his medicine."

"We'll check between here and the Reynolds' place." The sheriff glanced at his watch. "Should have another half hour of daylight to work with."

"My car's still over there. Can't move it until I find my keys." She made a move to stand.

Caleb took a step toward her. The real estate between them disappeared in two strides. "You're too weak. Matt can get your car as soon as we find your purse. For now, I'll give the Reynolds a call. Make sure they don't have it towed."

Caleb phoned his neighbor and gave a quick rundown of the situation. He asked if anyone had reported anything or found a purse.

They hadn't.

Caleb finished the call solemnly. There wasn't much to go on, and time ticked away.

"I feel like I should be doing something besides sitting here," Katherine said to the sheriff.

"Best thing you can do is wait it out. Let my

men do their work. I'll put out an AMBER Alert."
Sheriff Coleman shook her hand and then walked
to the door. "In the meantime, sit tight right here
in case I have more questions. Let me know if
anything else suspicious happens or you remember anything that might be important."

If Caleb heard things right, he'd just picked up
a houseguest. Couldn't say he was especially disappointed. "You'll call as soon as you hear anything, right?"

"You bet."

Caleb thanked the sheriff and walked him out
the door.

Outside, Caleb folded his arms. "What do you
think?"

Coleman scanned his notes. He rocked back on
his heels. "Not sure. Kids are most often taken by
a family member. Don't see many kidnappings.
Especially not out here."

"Doesn't sound good."

The sheriff dropped his gaze for a second and
shook his head.

"What are the chances of finding him alive?"

"The odds are better if he was taken by a rela-
tive. Doesn't sound like the case here." Coleman
broke eye contact. "That's a whole different ball
game."

The words were a sucker punch to Caleb's chest.

"I'd appreciate hearing any news or leads you

come across firsthand." Last thing Caleb wanted was for Katherine to learn what had happened to her nephew over the internet or on the news.

"Of course. There's always the possibility he got away and will turn up here. The first twenty-four hours are the most critical."

The thought of a little boy wandering around lost and alone in the dark woods clenched Caleb's gut. "Why'd they threaten to kill him if she called the police?"

"They probably want to keep this quiet. To scare her. Who knows? She's not a celebrity or politician. Why would someone target her? We need to find her phone. In the meantime, have her make a list of enemies. Ask her if she's gotten into a fight with anyone lately. Could someone have a problem with her or her sister? Without her cell, we don't know if anyone's trying to contact her to make demands."

Caleb shook Coleman's hand before he got in his cruiser and pulled away.

He stood on the porch for a long moment, looking out at the landscape that had kept him from getting too restless for years. He couldn't imagine living anywhere else. This was home. And yet, an uneasy feeling crept over him.

Chapter Three

Matt's black pickup roared down the drive. Caleb walked to meet his foreman. "Find anything?"

"There's nothing around for miles. Whoever did this got away fast."

The whole scenario seemed calculated, ruling out the slight possibility this was a case of mistaken identity. "You checked with the McGraths?"

Matt nodded. "They haven't seen or heard anything all day. Gave us the okay to search their property and barn. I sent Jimmy and Greg over to the Reynolds', too. Not a trace. No one saw anything, either. There's nothing but her word to go on." Worry showed in the tight muscles of his face. "I gotta ask. You think it's possible she could be making this up?"

Caleb ground his back teeth. "This is real. She has the bumps and bruises to prove it."

"It was a crappy question but needed to be asked. There's no trail to follow. No other signs she's telling the truth. Could the marks be from something else?"

"You didn't see her. The terror in her eyes. The blood. I had to cut her free from the fencing. Dig barbs out of her leg."

"Stay with me for a minute. I'm just sayin'. Where's the proof she even has a nephew? How do we know all the mechanical stuff upstairs is oiled and the cranks are working with her?"

The point was valid. If he hadn't been the one to find her, he might wonder if she was crazy, too. But he had been the one. Her tortured expression might haunt him for the rest of his life. She'd faced the hell in front of her with her chin up. He didn't doubt her. "I hear you and I understand your concerns. I do. But you're off base."

"How can you be so sure?"

"I just know."

Matt cocked one eyebrow. "Okay…how?"

"Call it gut instinct."

"Then I'll take your word for it. I'll give her a ride wherever she wants to go." He took a step toward the house.

"Sheriff wants her to stick around."

Matt hesitated. His doubt about the situation was written all over his face. To his credit, he seemed to know when to hold his tongue. He turned toward the barn. "Be careful. You have a tendency to get too involved with creatures that need saving. I'll check on the boys out back."

It would be dark before too long. The sun, a bright orange glow on the horizon, was retreating. "I'll put on a pot of coffee."

As soon as Caleb walked inside, Katherine hit him with the first question.

"What did the sheriff say?" She stroked the little yellow tabby who had made herself at home in her lap.

"How'd you manage that?" He inclined his chin toward the kitty.

She shrugged. "She hopped on the couch and curled up. She's a sweet girl. Why?"

"Claws has been afraid of people ever since I brought her into the house."

"How'd she lose her leg?"

"Found her like that when I was riding fences one day. She was in pretty bad shape. Vet fixed her up, and she's been my little shadow ever since. Scratched the heck out of Matt the first time he picked her up. Usually hides when I have company."

Claws purred as Katherine scratched under her chin. "Can't imagine who would hurt such a sweet girl." She paused, and then locked gazes. "You were going to tell me what the sheriff said."

"That he'd contact me if they found anything.

Do you remember what else you were doing before the men showed up?"

"We'd bought a jar of local honey. We were picking out pumpkins to take home with us."

"Anything else?"

"That's it. That's all I remember."

Caleb moved to the side table and picked up the empty soup bowl. "You drink coffee?"

"Yes."

"Give me five minutes. In the meantime, sheriff wants a list of names. Anyone who might've been out to hurt your sister. Or you."

He put down the bowl, took a pen and paper from a side table drawer and placed it next to her before moving into the kitchen.

She was making scribbles on the sheet of paper when he returned and handed her a cup. "Wasn't sure how you took yours."

"Black is fine." She gripped the mug. "What's next? How long does the sheriff expect me to sit here and do nothing?"

"Waiting's hard. Believe me, everything that can be done is happening. The authorities have all their resources on this. My men are filling the gaps. It's best to stay put until the sheriff calls. Give yourself a chance to heal. How's your leg?"

"Better. Thank you."

His bandage job looked to be holding. "What was the last thing you remembered before Noah was…" Damn. He hated saying the word *taken* out loud.

"I don't know. After the pumpkins, we were going on a hayride. I'd gone over to tell him. He was playing with the really big ones on the edge of the patch. Near the woods. I took pictures of him climbing on them. If we can find my phone, I can supply the sheriff with a recent photo."

"Think you might have captured the guys on your camera?"

"It's possible."

"I'll notify the sheriff."

Caleb phoned Coleman and provided an update. The hunt for her belongings intensified. They might find answers. At the very least, Matt would believe her if she could produce a picture of her nephew. Why did that seem so important?

"Think they saw you snapping shots?"

She shrugged. "Don't know."

"Did Noah scream?"

"They covered his mouth at the same time they grabbed him around the waist. Didn't bother once we got out of range." Sadness, desperation, fear played out across her features. "Please tell me we'll find him. I don't know what they want. If I can't produce a file, I'm afraid they'll take it out on him."

Caleb moved from his spot on the love seat to

the couch and draped an arm around her. "We won't allow it. We'll figure it out."

"I wish I'd been thinking more clearly. I panicked. Dropped everything. If I had those pics now, we might have a direction."

Five raps on the door—Matt's signature knock—came before the door sprang open. His foreman rushed in holding a black purse.

Claws darted under the sofa.

Katherine strained to push off the couch. "You found it."

"The boys did." Matt's gaze moved from Caleb to Katherine. His brow furrowed and a muscle along his jaw twitched.

"Any luck with my phone?"

"This is all we got before we ran out of daylight. All the men in the county are involved. A few want to keep going. The rest will pick up the search tomorrow."

Matt handed the bag to Katherine. She immediately dumped out the contents, palming Noah's pill bottle and inhaler.

"Did you let Coleman know?" Caleb asked.

Matt nodded. "Sure did. There's something else you should know. Thanks to that little bit of rain we got the other day, one of the boys located four-wheeler tracks on the McGrath farm on the other side of the fence near where you said you found her."

Matt couldn't deny she'd told the truth now.

Katherine was already digging around the large tote, tossing snack bags and juice boxes onto the sofa. "It all happened so fast. I can't even remember where I put my phone. I just remember taking photographs one minute, then the world spinning out of control the next. I wouldn't even believe any of this myself if it hadn't happened to me. I keep feeling like all of this is some kind of bad dream, and I'll wake up any second to find everything back to normal. Noah will be here with me. My sister will be alive."

As if shaking off the heavy thoughts, Katherine jammed her hand back inside her bag. Blood soaked through one section of the gauze on her leg.

"If you won't let me take you to the hospital, you'll have to listen to what I say. We have to keep this elevated." Caleb curled his fingers around her calf and lifted, watching for any signs he hurt her. Based on her grimace, her darkening eyes, she was winning the fight against the pain. When the shock and adrenaline wore off later, she'd be in for it. He didn't like the idea of her being home alone in Dallas when it happened.

"You're right. I'm sorry. I'm not thinking clearly. This whole ordeal has me scattered. Waiting it out will drive me insane."

Caleb didn't even want to think about the possibility of not finding her nephew.

Big violet eyes stared at him. "It's gone. I must've still been holding it. They have no way to contact me. What if they've called already? What if they've…"

"Sleep here tonight." Caleb ignored Matt's sharp intake of breath. He hadn't planned to make the offer. It just came out.

"I'D GET IN your way. Besides, you have plenty to do to keep busy without me underfoot," Katherine argued without conviction.

"If you stay here, I'll be able to keep an eye on your leg and get some work done."

Going back to her one-bedroom apartment was about as appealing as sleeping alone in a cave. Her keys were in her purse, but she doubted she could drive. Even though Noah had only been there a week, she couldn't face going home without him. Staying at the ranch, being this near Caleb, provided a measure of strength and comfort.

His warm brown eyes darkened. "I can have Margaret turn down the bed in the guest room. Doesn't make sense for you to go anywhere."

"I don't want to be rude. I just…"

Frustration, exhaustion was taking hold. It had been three long hours since the ordeal began.

"No reason to leave. This is best place to be for now."

Caleb seemed the type of guy who took care of anyone and everyone he came across. Cowboy code or something. Still, she didn't want to abuse his goodwill. "Thank you for everything you've done so far, but—"

"It's no trouble."

Matt ran the toe of his boot along the floor. "Think they'll call her house?"

"I saw no need for a landline."

The cowboy sat on the edge of the coffee table. "Then it's settled. You stay. Agreed?"

"For tonight."

Matt quickly excused himself and disappeared down the hall. What was that all about?

The cowboy followed.

Her heart gave a little skip at the satisfied smile on his face. She refocused on the sheet of paper. Who would want something from Leann? What file could she possibly have? A manila folder? Computer file?

Why on earth would they think Katherine had it? If they knew Leann at all, they'd realize she could keep a secret. The last thing she would do was confide in her sister.

Maybe a trip to Austin would help? She could start with Leann's computer.

She rubbed her temples to ease the pounding

between her eyes. Other than playing with the pumpkins, had Noah spoken to anyone? Had she?

There had to have been at least a dozen other people around. Were any of them in on it? A chill raced up her spine.

Caleb reappeared, holding a crutch. "I should take another look at that ankle before you put any weight on it."

"I just remembered something. There was a man talking to me while I was in line to buy tickets for the hayride."

His rich brown eyes lifted to meet hers and her heart faltered.

"He could've been there to distract you."

Panic at reliving the memory gripped her. She buried her face in her hands. "I'm so scared. What will they do to him?"

He cupped her chin, lifting her face until her eyes met his. "You can't think like that."

"He has to be terrified. He's so vulnerable and alone. I'm praying they haven't hurt him. He's been through so much already. I was supposed to take care of him. Protect him. Keep him safe."

"If he's half as strong as his aunt, he'll be all right." She could tell by his set jaw he meant it.

She almost laughed out loud. Little did he know how weak and miserable she felt, and her heart was fluttering with him so close, which could not be more inappropriate under the circumstances. "I promised on my sister's grave I would look after him. Look what I did."

The weight of those words sat heavier than a block of granite. Panic squeezed her chest. Her breath labored.

Brown eyes, rich, the color of newly turned fall leaves, set in an almost overwhelmingly attractive face stared at her. Before she could protest, his hand guided her face toward his shoulder.

"Don't blame yourself," he soothed. "Talk like that won't bring him back." His voice was a low rumble.

This close she could breathe in his scent. He smelled of fresh air and outdoors, masculine and virile. His mouth was so close to hers she could feel his cinnamon-scented breath on her skin.

She'd felt so alone, so guilty, and then suddenly this handsome cowboy was offering comfort.

Caleb pulled away too soon. Her mind was still trying to wrap itself around the fact a room could be charged with so much tension in less than a second, and in the next she could feel so guilty for allowing herself to get caught up in it.

The sounds of boots scuffling across tiles came from the other room. He inclined his chin toward the kitchen. "Sounds like we have company."

He stood and held out his hand.

By the time Katherine limped into the kitchen with Caleb's help, the table was filled with men.

As soon as they saw her, chatter stopped and they stood. There were half a dozen cowboys surrounding the table.

"Ma'am." Matt tipped his hat.

She smiled, nodded.

Caleb led her to the sink to wash her hands and blot her face with a cool, wet towel.

"Take my seat," he said, urging her toward the head of the table.

Matt leaned forward, staring, lips pinched together.

As soon as she thanked the cowboy and sat, conversation resumed.

He handed her a plate of ribs and beans. She smiled up at him to show her gratitude.

He brought her fresh iced tea before making his own fixings and seating himself at the breakfast bar.

She looked down the table at the few guys. These must be the boys he'd referred to earlier.

Yep, he took care of everyone around him, including her.

WHEN DINNER WAS over, Caleb excused himself and moved to the back porch. Remnants of Katherine's unique smell, a mix of spring flowers and vanilla, filled his senses when he was anywhere near her. He had to detach and analyze the situation. He needed a clear head. He could think outside.

Katherine had clearly been through hell. An un-expected death and a kidnapping within a week?

Before he could get too deep into that thought, the screen door creaked open and Matt walked out.

"Tough situation in there," he said, nodding to-ward the house.

"You believe her now?"

"Hard to dispute the evidence." He held his toothpick up to the light. "I didn't mean to insult her before. I didn't know what to believe."

"Can't say I wouldn't be suspicious, too, if I hadn't seen her moments after the fact."

"I know you're planning to help, and it's the right thing to do, but is there something going on between you two?"

He clamped his mouth shut. Shock momentarily robbed his voice.

"No. Of course not. I met her five minutes ago. What makes you think otherwise?"

"You have a history of getting involved with women in crisis."

"I'd help anyone who needed it."

"True."

Matt didn't have to remind him of what he al-ready knew. He had a knack for attracting women in trouble. Did he feel an attraction to Katherine? Yes. Was she beautiful? Yes. But he knew bet-ter than to act on it. The last time he'd rescued a woman, she'd returned the favor by breaking his heart. She'd let him help her, but then deserted him. He needed to keep his defenses up and not get involved with Katherine the way he did with the others. Period.

That being said, he wouldn't turn away a woman in trouble. Did this have something to do with his twisted-up childhood? He was pretty damn sure Freud would think so.

Tension tightened Matt's face. "Just be careful. When the last one walked out, she took a piece of you with her. You haven't been the same since."

"Not going to happen again."

Matt arched his brow. "If I'm honest, I'm also bothered by the fact there's a kid involved."

Figured. Caleb knew exactly what his friend was talking about. "My ex and her little girl have nothing to do with this."

"No? You sure about that?"

"I don't see how Katherine's nephew being kidnapped has anything to do with my past," Caleb said. Impatience edged his tone.

"A woman shows up at your door with a kid in crisis and you can't see anything familiar about it? I've known you a long time—"

"You don't have to remind me."

"Then you realize I wouldn't come out of the blue with something. I think your judgment's clouded." Matt's earnest eyes stared into Caleb. His buddy had had a ringside seat to the pain Cissy had caused when she'd walked out, taking Savannah with her. Matt's intentions were pure gold, if not his reasoning.

"I disagree." He couldn't deny or explain his attraction to Katherine. It was more than helping out a random person in need. He could be honest with himself. He probably felt a certain amount of pull toward her because of the child involved. No doubt, the situation tugged at his heart. But he'd only just met her. He'd help her. She'd leave. Whether she was wearing his favorite color on her underwear or not, they'd both move on. He had no intention of finding out if the pale blue lace circled her tiny waist. He was stubborn, not stupid. "Nothing else matters until we find that little guy."

"Saw the sheriff earlier." Matt's hands clenched. "Heard about the boy having a medical condition. What kind of person would snatch a little kid like that?"

Matt didn't use the word *monster,* but Caleb knew his buddy well enough to know he thought it.

"That's what I plan to find out."

"You know I'll help in any way I can. Then she can go home, and you can get on with your life."

Caleb chewed on a toothpick. "How are the men taking everything?"

"Hard. Especially with Jimmy's situation. He's still out searching."

"Meant to ask how his little girl's doing when I saw him tonight."

Matt shook his head. "Not good."

Damn. "Send 'em home. They need to be with their families."

"I think most of them want to be here to keep searching. Jimmy made up flyers. A few men headed into town to put the word out. Everyone wants to help with the search. They're working out shifts to sleep."

"Tell 'em how much I appreciate their efforts. We'll do everything we can to make sure this boy comes home safe. And we won't stop looking for him until we do."

Matt nodded, his solemn expression intensifying when he said, "You be careful with yourself, too."

"This is not like the others."

"You don't know that yet," Matt said, deadpan.

Caleb bit back his response. Matt's heart was in the right place. "Tell Gus I can't meet tomorrow. I know the buyer wants to stop by, but I can't."

"This is the third time he's set up a meeting. You haven't liked anyone he's found so far."

"Can't dump my mare on the first person that strolls in."

"Or the second…or third apparently. Every time we breed her, the same thing happens. It's been three years and not one of her foals has lived."

"Which is exactly the reason I don't want to sell her. What will end up happening to her when they realize she can't produce? Besides, she's useful around here."

"How so? The men use four-wheelers so it won't do any good to assign her to one of them. I have my horse and you have yours."

"I'll find more for her to do. Dawn's getting older. I'll use both. Not all lost causes are lost causes."

Matt's eyebrow rose as he turned toward the barn. "We'll see."

CALEB HAD BEEN buried in paperwork for a couple hours when Katherine appeared in his office doorway, leaning on the crutch.

"Mind some company?"

She wore an oversize sleep shirt and loose-fitting shorts cinched above the hips. Even clothes two sizes too big couldn't cloak her sexy figure. Her soft curves would certainly get a man fantasizing about what was beneath those thin threads.

"Sure. Where'd you get the clothes?"

"Margaret put these on the bed with a note saying they belonged to her daughter. Even said I could borrow them as long as I needed to. I managed to clean up without getting my leg wet. I took a nap. I'm feeling much better."

Katherine sat in the oversize leather chair Caleb

loved. It was big enough for two. Claws hopped up a second later, curling in her lap.

"Any word from the sheriff yet?"

"No. I put in a call to him. Should hear back any minute. If your leg is feeling better in the morning, I thought we could head to Austin."

"I want to stay here and search for my phone."

"We'll look first. Then we'll head out. Any chance you have a copy of your sister's keys?"

"Afraid not."

"We'll get in anyway."

She cocked her head and pursed her lips. "Tell me not to ask why you know how to break in someone's house."

Caleb cracked a smile as he rubbed his temples. "Misspent youth. Besides, some secrets a man takes to his grave." He chuckled. "I've been thinking. You have any idea if Noah's father knew about him?"

Katherine heaved a sigh, twirling her fingers through Claws's fur. "I should but don't. My sister's relationships were complicated. Especially ours."

"Families can be tricky," Caleb agreed.

"When our parents got in the car crash my freshman year of college, I resented having to come home to take care of her." Katherine dropped her gaze. "I probably made everything worse. Did everything wrong."

"Not an easy situation to be thrown into."

Katherine's lips trembled but no tears came.

"Leann had always been something of a free spirit. Her life was lived without a care in the world. I was the one who stressed over grades and stayed home on Friday nights to study or to help out around the house. My parents owned a small business and worked long hours. I was used to being alone. Leann, on the other hand, was always out with friends. The two of us couldn't have been more opposite. Sometimes I wished I could have been more like her. Instead, I came down on her hard. Tried to force her to be more like me."

"You had no choice but to be serious. Sounds like you were the one who had to grow up." She was a survivor who coped the best way she could.

"What about your parents?" She turned the tables.

"My mom was a saint. The man who donated sperm? A jerk. Dad, if you can call him that, didn't treat my mother very well before he decided to run out." Caleb's story was the same one being played out in every honky-tonk from there to the border. "I rebelled. I was angry at her for allowing him to hurt her when he was here. Angry with myself for not jumping in to save her. Mom worked herself too hard to pay the bills. Didn't have insurance. Didn't take care of her diabetes. Died when I was fifteen." The familiar stab of anger and regret punctured him.

"Did you blame yourself?"

"I know a thing or two about feeling like you let someone down. Only hurt yourself with that kind of thinking, though. I found the past is better left there. Best to focus on the here and now. Do that well and the future will take care of itself."

"Is that your way of saying I should let go?"

"I did plenty of things wrong when I was a child. You could say I was a handful. Dwelling on it doesn't change what was."

She studied the room. "Looks like you're making up for it now."

Pride filled his chest. "Never felt like I belonged anywhere before here." He'd been restless lately though. Matt had said Caleb missed having little feet running around. The wounds were still raw from Cissy leaving. Another reason he should keep a safe distance from the woman curled up on his favorite chair. She looked as though she belonged there. "TorJake is a great home."

"I love the name. How'd you come up with it?"

"My first big sale was a beautiful paint horse. The man who'd sold him to me when he was a pony said he tore up the ground like no other. He'd been calling him Specdy Jake. I joked that I should enter him over at Lone Star Park as

ToreUpTheEarthJake. Somehow, his nickname got shortened to TorJake, and it stuck. Had to geld him early on to keep his temperament under control. He had the most interesting, well-defined markings I've ever seen. Sold him to a bigwig movie producer in Hollywood to use filming a Western. The sale allowed me to buy neighboring farms and eventually expand to what I have now."

"Was it always your dream to own a horse ranch?"

"I figured I'd end up in jail or worse. When I landed a job at my first working ranch, I fell in love. A fellow by the name of Hank was an old pro working there. He taught me the ropes. Said he saw something in me. He never had kids of his own. Told me he went to war instead. Became a damn good marine. Special ops. He taught me everything I know about horse ranches and keeping myself out of trouble."

"Where is he now?"

"He passed away last year."

"I'm so sorry." Her moment of distraction faded too fast, and he knew what she was thinking based on the change in her expression. "You don't think they'll hurt him, do you?"

He ground his back teeth. "I hope not. I don't like this situation for more than the obvious reasons. This whole thing feels off. Your sister dies a week ago. Now this with Noah. Could the two be connected somehow?"

Katherine gasped. Her hand came up to cover her mouth. "I didn't think about how odd the timing is."

"Maybe she got in a fight with Noah's father. Was about to reveal who he was. He could be someone prominent. Most missing children are taken by family members or acquaintances, once you rule out runaways, according to the sheriff."

"Then what about the file?"

"I was thinking about that. Could be a paternity test."

"If his father took him, at least Noah will be safe, right?" Katherine threaded her fingers through her hair, pulling it off her face.

"It's possible. I don't mean any disrespect. Do you think it's possible your sister was blackmailing him?"

"He didn't pay child support. That much I know. I paid her tuition. She enrolled in a social program to help with Noah's care. Got him into a great daycare. I was planning to move to Austin in a few months to be closer. I work for a multinational software company scheduling appointments for our trainers to visit customer sites, so it doesn't matter where I live. I wanted to be close so I could help out more. I can't help wondering what kind of person would hurt the mother of his child."

"I'm probably grasping at straws. We'll start with trying to figure out who he is. See what happens there."

"She was reckless before Noah. I thought her life was on track since his diagnosis. She got a part-time job at a coffee shop and enrolled in community college. She reconnected with me."

His ring tone cut into the conversation. "It's Matt." He brought the phone to his ear. "What's the word?"

"Jimmy found two things out at the Reynolds' place. A stuffed rabbit and a cell. I told him to meet me at your place."

"I appreciate the news. We'll keep watch for you."

Caleb hit End and told Katherine what his ranch hand had found.

"I hope I got a shot of someone. They wore dark sunglasses, so their faces might be hard to make out, but maybe I captured someone else involved. Like the man who distracted me."

"Either way, we'll know in a minute." Wouldn't do any good to set false expectations. And yet, hope was all she had.

Looking into her violet eyes, damned if he wasn't the one who wanted to put it there.

A knock at the door had him to his feet faster

than he could tack a horse, and tossing a throw blanket toward Katherine.

Caleb led Jimmy and Matt into the study. After a quick introduction, Jimmy advanced toward Katherine, carrying a phone. "Found this along the tree line by the Reynolds' place. Look familiar?"

"Yes, thank you. That looks like mine." Katherine's eyes sparkled with the first sign of optimism since Caleb had found her in the woods. She checked the screen. "Seven missed calls and a voice mail."

Another knock sounded at the door. Caleb walked Sheriff Coleman into the study a moment later, before moving to her side. The hope in her eyes was another hint of light in the middle of darkness and blackness, and every worst fear realized.

"Put it on speaker."

"I'm praying the message is from the kidnappers, but I'm scared it's them, too."

Caleb tensed. "Whatever's on that phone, we'll deal with it."

Her gaze locked on to his as she held up the cell and listened.

"What's wrong with the boy? You have twenty-four hours to help me figure it out and get me the file. I'll call back with instructions. No more games. Think about it. Tick. Tock."

Click.

Caleb took the phone and scanned the log. "Private number." He looked at Coleman. "There any way to trace this call?"

"Doubt it. They're probably smart enough to use a throwaway. We'll check anyway." Coleman scribbled fresh notes. "You mentioned the file before. Has anything come to mind since we last spoke?"

Katherine shook her head. "I've been guessing they mean a computer file, but I'm not positive. It could be anything."

Outside, gravel spewed underneath tires. Caleb moved to the window. Two dark SUVs with blacked-out windows came barreling down the drive. "Sheriff, you tell anybody you were coming here?"

Coleman shook his head. "Didn't even tell my dispatcher."

Katherine's eyes pleaded. She wrapped the blanket around her tighter, clutching the stuffed rabbit Jimmy had handed her. "I don't have the first clue what file they're talking about. As soon as they realize it, they'll kill us both. Don't let them near me."

"Dammit. They must've followed someone here. The sheriff can cover for us." Caleb pulled Katherine to her feet as she gripped her handbag. He moved to the kitchen door, stopping long enough for her to slip on her sandals before looking back at his men.

"Can you cover me?"

Chapter Four

Caleb's arm, locked like a vise around Katherine's waist, was the only thing holding her upright.

The barn wasn't far but any slip, any yelp, and the men would barrel down on them. The lightest pressure on her leg caused blood to pulse painfully down her calf. She breathed in through her nose and out through her mouth, slowly, trying to keep her breaths equal lengths and her heart rate calm.

Could the darkness cloak them? Hide them from the danger not a hundred yards away?

Katherine squinted.

The glow from lamplight illuminated the parking pad. There were two men. Dark suits. A wave of déjà vu slammed into her like a hard swell.

They weren't close enough to make out facial features. Only stature. They looked like linebackers. Had the man with the jagged scar etched in his overly tanned face come back to kill her? He would haunt her memory forever.

Her pulse hammered at the recollection. "Even

if you have a car stashed here somewhere, they'll never let us get past them."

"Don't need to."

"If you have another plan besides trying to barrel through them, or sneak around them, I'm all ears." She glanced at her bad leg and frowned.

"You still have your keys?"

She nodded. tucking the rabbit into her purse.

"Then we'll take your car."

"How will we do that? It's too far. I doubt I could get there unless you carried me." He seemed perfectly able to do just that.

"Won't have to. You'll see why." Caleb leaned her against the side of a tree near the back door of the barn. "Wait here."

She didn't want to be anywhere else but near him.

A moment later he pushed an ATV next to her. A long-barreled gun extended from his hand. A rifle? Katherine wouldn't know a shotgun from an AK-47. She only knew the names of those two from watching TV.

"This'll get us there." He patted the seat.

She glided onto the back with his help.

He slid a powerful leg in front of her and gripped the bars. "I think we're far enough away. The barn should block some of the noise. Hang on tight just in case they hear us."

Katherine clasped her hands around his midsection. His abdominal muscles were rock-solid. Was there a weak spot on his body? She allowed his strength to ease the tension knotting her shoulders. His warmth to calm her shaking arms.

"Why would they come looking for me? They said I had twenty-four hours. Why come after me before that?"

"Might be afraid you'll alert the authorities, or disappear. Plus, they must've figured out your nephew needs medication since they asked what was wrong with him."

"How did they find me?"

"There weren't many places to look other than my ranch."

"Good point." She hated the thought of putting Caleb and his men in danger. At least the sheriff was there to defend them. He would have questions for the men in the SUV. He'd slow the plans of any attackers and keep Caleb's crew safe. A little voice reminded her how the kidnappers had warned her about police involvement. She prayed Sheriff Coleman's presence didn't create a problem for Noah.

The trip was short and bumpy but allowed enough time for her eyes to adjust to the dark. Caleb cut the engine well before the clearing as she dug around in her purse for the keys.

"They might be watching your car, so we'll need to play this the right way." His earnest brown eyes intent on her, radiating confidence, were all she could see clearly in the dark.

A shiver cycled through her nerves, alighting her senses. It was a sensual feeling she was becoming accustomed to being this close to him. It spread warmth through her, and she felt a pull toward him stronger than the bond between nucleons in an atom. His quiet strength made her feel safe.

Caleb's powerful arms wrapped around her, and she wanted to melt into him and disappear. *Not now.* She canceled the thought. Noah needed her. No amount of stress or fear would make her shrink. She would be strong so she could find him. Sheer force of will had her pushing forward.

"Wait here." Caleb moved pantherlike from the tree line. Stealth. Intentional. Deadly. His deliberate movements told her there wasn't much this cowboy had faced he couldn't handle.

Katherine scanned the dark parking lot. She couldn't see far but figured even a second's notice would give Caleb a chance to react.

There was no one.

Nothing.

Except the din of the woods behind her. Around her. Surrounding her. A chilling symphony of chirping and sounds of the night.

Silently she waited for the all-clear or the telltale blast of his gun. For a split second she considered making a run for it. Maybe she could give her-self up and beg for mercy before it was too late? Maybe the men would take her to Noah, and she could get his medicine to him now that she had her purse back?

Maybe they would take what they wanted and kill her?

They'd been ruthless so far. She had no doubt they would snap her neck faster than a branch if given the chance. Without his medicine, Noah would be dead, too.

All her hopes were riding on the unexpected hero cowboy, but what if he didn't come back? What if he disappeared into the night and ended up injured, bleeding out or worse?

Caleb was strong and capable, but he had no idea what kind of enemy they were up against. A bullet didn't discriminate between good and evil.

When the interior light of her car clicked on, she realized she'd been holding her breath. Ca-leb's calm voice coaxed her.

Another wave of relief came when she slid into the passenger side and secured her seat belt. He put the car in Reverse and backed out of the parking space. The sound of gravel spinning under tires had never sounded so much like heaven.

"You did good." His words were like a warm blanket around her frayed nerves.

"Thank you. Think it's safe to call the ranch?"

He nodded, stopping the car at the edge of the lot. The phone was to his ear a second later. He said a few uh-huhs into the receiver before ending the call and getting on the road. "Everyone's fine. Two men showed up, asking questions."

"What did they want?"

"They flashed badges. Said they were government investigators following a lead on a corporate fraud scheme."

A half laugh, half cough slipped out. "Leann? She didn't even have a normal job. She worked at a coffee shop."

"They didn't ask for your sister. They asked if someone matching your description had been seen in the area."

Fear pounded her chest. "Me? Corporate fraud? I don't have the first idea what they're talking about. I'm a scheduler for a software company. That's a far cry from a spy."

"Coleman took their information and plans to follow up through proper channels. Maybe the trail will lead somewhere."

"I hope so. Where do we go in the meantime?"

"Your sister's place. What's the address?"

Katherine scrolled through her contacts and read the details while he programmed the GPS in her car.

"We can check her computer and talk to her friends. Maybe we'll find answers there."

"Or just more questions. I told you. Knowing my sister, this won't be easy. I'm not sure who she hung around with let alone what she might've gotten herself into that could lead to this."

"Maybe the sheriff will come up with something. Good thing he was there. Might make these men think twice before they do anything else."

"Or…" She could've said it might make them kill Noah but didn't. No police. They'd been clear as day about it. Had she just crossed a line and put her nephew in more danger? Damn.

"They won't hurt him," Caleb said as though he read her thoughts.

"How can you be so sure?"

His grip tightened on the steering wheel. His jaw clenched. His gaze remained steady on the road in front of them. "We can't afford to think that way. First things first, let's get to Austin. We'll take the rest as it comes. Send Coleman the photos you took of Noah earlier."

"I almost forgot I had these." She scrolled through the pictures from the pumpkin patch. Noah smiled as he climbed on top of a huge orange gourd and exclaimed himself "king." Tremors vibrated from her chest to her neck. A stab of guilt pierced her. She scrutinized other details in the picture. Nothing but yellow-green grass and brown trees. A frustrated sigh escaped. "No good.

I can't make anything out on the small screen except him and a couple of large pumpkins."

"Look up the last number I dialed, and send Coleman every shot you took today. He can blow them up and get a better view."

Her heart lurched as she shared the pictures one by one. When she was finished, she shut her eyes.

Caleb took her hand and squeezed. Warmth filled her, comforting her. When was the last time a man's touch did that?

She searched her memory but found nothing. No one, aside from Caleb, had ever had that effect on her.

"Think you can get a little shut-eye?"

Kathcrine was afraid to close her eyes. Feared she'd relive the horror of seeing a screaming Noah being ripped from her arms over and over again. "Probably not."

"Lean your seat back a little."

She did as she watched out the window instead. Interstate 35 stretched on forever. Every minute that ticked by was a reminder Noah was slipping away. Waco came and went, as did a few other smaller towns. The exhaustion of the day wore her nerves thin. Sleep would come about as fast as Christmas to June, but she closed her eyes anyway, praying a little rest would rejuvenate her and help her think clearly. Maybe there was something obvious she was overlooking that could help her put the pieces together.

Had Leann said anything recently? Dropped any hints? Given any clue that might foreshadow what was to come?

Nothing popped into Katherine's thoughts. Besides, if she knew one thing about her sister, Leann could keep a secret.

Sadness pressed against her chest, tightening her muscles. Leann must've known something was up. Why hadn't she said anything? Had she been in trouble? Maybe Katherine could've helped.

Katherine tried to remember the exact words her sister had used when she'd asked if Noah could come to Dallas for a week. Katherine could scarcely remember their conversation let alone expect perfect recall. How sad was that?

Her sister was dead, and Katherine couldn't even summon up the final words spoken between them. Guilt and regret ate at her conscience. Wait. There'd been a tornado warning, which was odd for October. When she joked about not being able to trust Texas weather, Leann had issued a sigh.

Katherine sat upright. "She knew something bad was going to happen."

"I figured it was the reason she sent Noah to stay with you."

"That means everything she did was premeditated. Maybe she'd gotten mixed up in a bad deal she didn't know how to get out of. But what?"

"Drugs?"

"No. She might have been a handful, but she didn't even drink alcohol."

Caleb shrugged. "My mind keeps circling back to the father."

"I guess it could be. I can't think of anyone else who would have so much to lose. Then again, I didn't know my sister very well as an adult. I believe she realized something was about to happen. That's as much as I can count on." Would Leann have blackmailed someone? Didn't sound right to Katherine. Her sister had always been a bit reckless, but not mean-spirited.

She was untrustworthy. Katherine had never been able to depend on her sister. A painful memory burst through her thoughts....

Leann was supposed to watch Katherine's dog, Hero, while Katherine had been away on a school trip. Leann had sneaked him to the park off-leash to catch a Frisbee after Katherine had said no. He'd followed the round disc far into the brush and never come back out. The whole time Katherine had been gone, she'd had no idea her dog was missing.

He'd been gone for three days by the time Katherine returned home. She hadn't cared. She'd looked for him anyway. She'd searched the park, the area surrounding the open field, and the woods, but he was nowhere to be found.

Losing Hero had delivered a crushing blow to Katherine.

It was the last time she'd allowed her sister around anything she cared about.

She sighed. When it came to Leann, just about anything was possible.

"We don't have any other leads. It's a good place to start."

She wanted—no, needed—to believe her sister wasn't capable of spite. Leann had always been a free thinker. She was Bohemian, a little eccentric, not a calculated criminal. Especially not the type to hold on to hate or to try to hurt someone else.

Desperation nearly caved Katherine.

"We'll find the connection and put this behind you." Caleb's words were meant to comfort her. They didn't.

They would be at Leann's place soon and there had to be something there to help them. Get to the apartment. Find whatever it is the men want. Exchange the file for Noah. Mourn her sister. Try to forget this whole ordeal happened. *If only life were so easy.*

The hum of the tires on the highway coupled with the safety of being with someone who had her back for once allowed her to relax a little. Maybe she could lay her head back and drift off. Adrenaline had faded, draining her reserves.

She closed her eyes for at least an hour before the GPS told them to turn left. "Destination is on the right."

Katherine's heart skipped. In two hundred feet, a murderer might be waiting. Or the ticket to saving her nephew. Oh, God, it had to be there. Otherwise, she had nothing.

Caleb pulled his gun from the floorboard as he drove past the white two-story apartment building.

The GPS recalculated. "Make the next legal U-turn."

He pressed Stop. "We better not risk walking in the front door. We don't know who might be waiting on the other side."

Good point. "There's a back stairwell. We can go through the kitchen entrance."

Even long past midnight on a weekday, the streets and sidewalks teamed with college students milling around. Activity buzzed as groups of twos and threes crisscrossed the road into the night. Music thumped from backyards. Lights were strung outside. It would be easy to blend into this environment.

He put the car in Park a few buildings down from Leann's place. "We can walk from here. But first, I want to check in with Matt."

Katherine agreed. She had no idea what waited for her at her sister's. Her stomach was tied in knots.

"Matt's voice mail picked up." Caleb closed the phone. "I'm setting my phone to vibrate. You might want to do the same."

"Great idea." Katherine numbly palmed her phone. She stared at the metal rectangle for a long moment, half afraid, half daring it to ring. In one second, it had the power to change her life forever and she knew it. *Think of something else. Anything.*

Caleb took her hand. She followed him through the dark shadows, fighting against the pain shooting through her leg.

He stopped at the bottom of the stairwell and mouthed, "Stay here."

"No." Katherine shook her head for emphasis.

"Let me check it out first. I'll signal when it's okay."

"What if someone's out here watching?" Katherine didn't want to let her cowboy out of her sight. She'd never been this scared, and if he broke the link between them, she was certain all her confidence would dissipate. "I want to go with you. Besides, you don't know what you're looking for."

His eyes were intense. Dark. Pleading. "I don't like taking risks with you."

She couldn't let herself be swayed. They might

not have much time inside, and she wouldn't wait out here while he did all the heavy lifting. "Either way, I'm coming."

Looking resigned, Caleb's jaw tightened. "You always this stubborn?"

"Determined. And I've never had this much on the line before."

His tense stance didn't ease. Instead he looked poised for battle. His grip tightened on her hand. His other hand was clenched around the barrel of a gun.

"Then let's go," he said.

Katherine stayed as close behind as she could manage, ignoring the thumping pain in her leg.

Caleb turned at the back door and mouthed, "No lights."

The streetlight provided enough illumination to see clearly. He turned the handle and the door opened. It should have been locked.

Hope of finding anything useful dwindled. Of course, the men would have come here first.

If there was anything useful around, wouldn't they have found it already? They couldn't have, she reminded herself. Or she and Noah would be dead.

She moved to the dining space. The small corner desk was stacked with papers. A photo of Leann holding baby Noah brought tears to her eyes. She blinked them back, tucking the keepsake in her purse. The laptop Katherine had bought Leann for school was nowhere in sight.

Caleb's sure, steady movements radiated calm Katherine wanted to cling to. She dug through the pile of papers neatly stacked on the dining-room table while Caleb worked through the room, examining papers and objects.

Luck had never smiled on Katherine. She had no idea why this capable cowboy appeared. She needed him. The feeling was foreign to her and yet it felt nice to lean on someone else for a change. He looked every bit the man who could hold her up, too.

The realization startled her.

She knew very little about him, and yet he'd become her lifeline in a matter of hours. She could scarcely think about doing this without him and she wasn't sure which thought scared her the most. Katherine got through life depending on herself.

"Find anything useful?" he asked from across the room.

"No. It's hard to see in the dark though. You think whoever was here got what they wanted?"

Caleb moved to her. "Hard to say. You haven't been here since before the funeral, right?"

Katherine nodded. "I offered to pick up Noah, but she said no. Come to think of it, she's the one who mentioned meeting halfway. She'd never suggested that before. She wanted to meet in Waco this time in a restaurant that was way off the interstate. I figured it was just Leann being herself. Wanting to try something new."

"Looking back, did she act strange or say anything else that sticks out?"

"When we met she looked stressed. Cagey. I thought the responsibility of caring for Noah might be getting to her. Don't get me wrong, she loved that little boy. But caring for any kid, let alone one with medical needs, is stressful. Even so, she was a better parent than I ever would be."

She could feel his physical presence next to her before his arm slipped around her shoulders. "You would have been fine. And you will be, once we get Noah back safely."

Easy for him to say. He didn't know her. She didn't want to dwell on her shortcomings. Not now. She'd have time enough to examine those later when this was all over and her nephew was safe. "I thought she needed a break. The responsibility was becoming a burden. And then I didn't even think twice when I found out she'd had an accident climbing. I just assumed she'd been reckless." A sob escaped. "What does that say about me?"

"That you're human."

"Or I'm clueless. No wonder she didn't trust me with the truth. She must've known how little faith I had in her."

He guided her chin up until her gaze lifted to meet his.

"When people tell you who they are, it's best to believe them."

"What if they change?"

"Only time can tell that. Besides, it never does any good chasing what-if. You have to go on the information you have. Move from there."

"I guess."

"Look. You're strong. Brave. Determined. You were doing right by your sister. She trusted you or she never would have sent Noah to stay with you. As for the restaurant, she might've been worried she was being followed. She might've had a hunch there'd be trouble. I'm guessing she didn't bet on anything of this magnitude. She must've thought with Noah safe, she could handle whatever came her way."

His words were like a bonfire on a cold night. Warm. Soothing. Comforting.

Katherine reached up on her tiptoes and kissed his cheek.

A LIGHT TOUCH from those silky lips and a hot trail lit from the point of contact. Caleb's fingers itched to get lost in that chestnut mane of hers. She slicked her tongue over those lips and his body reacted with a mind of its own. His blood heated to boiling. He swallowed hard. Damn.

One look into Katherine's eyes and he could see she was hurt and alone. He wouldn't take advantage of the situation even though every muscle in his body begged to lay her down right then and give her all the comfort and pleasure she could handle. Another time. Another place. Might be a different story?

Then again, he'd never been known for his timing. He'd taken Becca in when she'd showed up at his door in trouble. Anger still flared through him when he thought about the bruises on her face and her busted lip. No way would he turn away a woman who looked as though she'd been abused. Caring for her and giving her a place to stay until she got on her feet had been the right thing to do. Having a relationship was a bad idea.

He'd opened his home and developed feelings for her. *Look how that turned out,* a little voice in his head said. She'd left after a year, saying she needed time to figure herself out.

Katherine faced a different problem. She was being brave as hell facing it rather than running and hiding. "Let's see what else is here."

"While I'm here, I should find some clothes and change."

Caleb walked away. If he hadn't, he couldn't have been held responsible for his actions. His body wanted Katherine. He was a man. She lit fires in him with a slight touch. A spark that in-

"What happened between the two of you?" He doubted she'd tell him but he took a chance and asked anyway.

Katherine sat for a moment. She leaned forward, allowing him to deepen the pressure on her neck and move his hands to her shoulders.

"She was fifteen. Rebellious. There was this one time I specifically told her not to go out. I needed her home to let a repairman in. She didn't listen and left anyway. Probably out of spite. We had to go the night without A/C in the middle of a Dallas summer. I'd been in class all day and then worked the afternoon shift as a hostess. I was hot. Miserable. I decided to wait up for her. The minute she waltzed through the door, I blew up. Told her she was a spoiled brat."

"You had every right to ask her to pitch in more. It wasn't like you asked her to gut a hog."

"I didn't 'ask' anything. I demanded she stay home. I thought it was my job to tell her what to do with our parents gone, not that she made it easy. She didn't want to listen and was never there when I needed her. I resented her. I learned pretty fast that I couldn't depend on her and had to learn to do things on my own."

"You should be proud of yourself."

"I could've been more sympathetic. But Leann did what she did best—disappeared. When she came home, I noticed she'd been drinking. I came down on her too hard."

Caleb knew all about self-recrimination. Hadn't he been beating himself up with worry since his last girlfriend left? Hadn't the ache in his chest been a void so large he didn't think he'd ever fill it again?

Caleb increased pressure, working a knot out of Katherine's shoulder.

A self-satisfied smile crossed his lips at the way her silky skin relaxed under his touch, and for the little moan that escaped before she could quash it. "You always this tough on yourself?"

Katherine hugged her knees into her chest. "A week later when she left, she didn't come back. I didn't hear from her for years."

Caleb couldn't imagine how difficult it was for Katherine to say those words out loud. She couldn't be more than twenty-six or twenty-seven, and seemed keenly aware of all her misjudgments now. A few years younger than him, she bore the weight of the world on her shoulders. The knots he'd been working so hard to release tightened. "Your sister was old enough to know better. You were trying to do what was best. I'm sure she knew that on some level."

"No. I had to close myself off because it was too painful repeatedly being disappointed by her. We stopped speaking. I didn't hear from her again until this year. Noah had barely turned four. I didn't even know I had a nephew before then."

Caleb moved to face her and took a knee, reaching out to place her hand in his. Her skin was finer than silk, her body small and delicate. The point where skin made contact sent a jolt of heat coursing through him. "Life threw you for a loop, too. Besides, you did what any good person would. You stepped up to fill impossible shoes and did your best. Because you weren't perfect doesn't mean you failed. You're an amazing woman."

He looked at her, really looked at her. There was enough light to see a red blush crawl up her neck, reaching her cheeks. Her skin glowed, her eyes glittered. The fire in her eyes nothing in comparison to the one she lit inside him.

He studied the soft curves of her lush mouth and then let his gaze lower to the swell of her firm, pointed breasts. All he felt was heat. Heat and need. Her jeans, balanced low on slim hips, teased him with a sliver of skin between the edge and the bottom of her T-shirt. Damn that she was even sexier when she was hurting. He pulled on all the strength he had so as not to take her lips right there…then her body.

Caleb needed to redirect his thoughts before he allowed his hormones to get out of hand. She made it difficult to focus on anything but thoughts of how good her body would feel moving beneath his. Alter the circumstances and things might have been different. Last thing Caleb needed was to get tangled up with another woman who showed up at his door with a crisis. He pushed all sexual thoughts out of his psyche.

"Since there's nothing here, we'd better go. I'm actually surprised no one's been watching the place."

Her gaze darted around the room. "Where do we go next? We can't go back to your ranch, can we?"

"No. I don't want to put my men at risk any more than we already have. What about your place? Any chance Leann passed a file to you in Noah's things?"

Hope once again brimmed in her shimmering eyes. "I hadn't thought of that. It's a possibility."

Caleb glanced at his watch, ignoring the ache in his chest for her. "If we leave now, we'll make it before daylight."

He preferred to move under the cover of night anyway.

She pulled back as they started toward the door. "Wait."

Caleb eased more of her weight on him, ignoring the pulsing heat on his outer thigh at the point of contact. "What is it?"

"I want to grab more medicine and something

from Noah's room first." Katherine pushed off him to regain balance.

Her phone vibrated and she froze.

"Take a deep breath and then pick up," Caleb said.

She exhaled and answered.

"Is he breathing?" She paused. "Good. He has asthma. There's an inhaler he uses and I have medicine. I can bring them wherever—"

The guy on the line must've interrupted because Katherine became quiet again and just listened. "What time?"

Her expression vacillated between anger and panic.

"Where?" She signaled to Caleb for a pen and paper.

He retrieved them and watched as she jotted down "Sculpture at CenterPark" and then ended the call.

Her wide-eyed gaze flew up to him. "They want to meet tomorrow afternoon."

"Did they mention anything about the file we're looking for?"

She shook her head. "They only said to bring it to NorthPark Center."

"Good, it's out in the open. What time?"

"Three o'clock."

Caleb glanced at his watch. "We have plenty of time to check it out first."

"They told me to come alone." Determination thinned her lips before she turned and walked away.

He wouldn't argue as he closely followed her, ready to grab her if she faltered. She was determined to walk on her own; he'd give her that. The way she did "stubborn" was sexy as hell. Now was not the time for the conversation he needed to have with her. The one that said no way in hell was he allowing her to go by herself.

"Before we leave, is there any place we haven't looked? Did she have a secret hiding spot?"

"None she would share with me." As she moved behind the sofa, she stopped suddenly. "I didn't think about this before, but it makes perfect sense. We might not find anything, but it's worth checking out."

Katherine limped down the short hall and into the master bedroom.

She stopped in the middle of the room and looked up at the ceiling fan. "She had a small diary when we were kids that she hid by taping it to the top of one the blades. I found it when I was helping my parents spring clean once." A hint of sadness darkened her features. "Found out just how much she was sick of me when I peeked at the pages."

Caleb righted a chair that had been tossed

upside down and settled it in the center of the room. "Let me look."

Even on the chair, he couldn't see the tops of the half-dozen blades.

Puffs of dust floated down when he wiped the first. More of the same on the second. His hand stopped on a small rectangle on the third. "I found something."

"Can you tell what?" Her voice brightened with hope.

"It's secure." He didn't want to take a chance on damaging it by ripping it off. His fingers moved around the smooth surface. Tape? He peeled the sticky layer off the item. "I'll be damned. It's a cell phone."

"Thank God, they missed it."

"I don't recognize the brand," he said as he palmed it.

"Think it works?"

He pressed the power button. "It's dead. If we can find a store that sells these, we can buy a new cable or battery. We'll look up the manufacturer when we get back in the car."

"Okay." She spun around. "Oh, and I need to find something else."

He followed her down the hall to Noah's bedroom.

"I know it's here somewhere," she said, tossing around toys and clothes.

"What are you looking for? I'll help."

"No. I found it." She held up a stuffed reindeer. "It's Prancer. One of Noah's favorites. He apparently used to sleep with it all the time. Now he's into the rabbit. I was just thinking he'll need as many of his things as possible to make my place feel like home." She gathered a few more toys from the mess.

"Prancer? Seems like an interesting choice for a name. I mean, why not Rudolph?" He examined the stuffed animal.

"Noah thinks the other reindeer get overlooked. Said Rudolph gets all the glory," she said, melancholy.

Caleb couldn't help but crack a smile. "How old did you say he is?"

"Four."

"Sounds like a compassionate boy." He tucked the stuffed animal under his arm. "We'll keep Prancer safe until he's back with Noah."

When Caleb looked at her, his heart dropped. A dozen emotions played across her delicate features. Fear. Regret. Anxiety.

He walked to her and took her hand in his.

"We'll find him. I promise."

Before he could debate his actions, he tilted his head forward and pressed his lips to hers gently. The soft kiss intensified when she parted her lips to allow him access. His mouth covered hers as he swallowed her moan.

Both his hands cupped her cheeks, tilting her face until his tongue delved more deeply, tasting her.

She pulled back long enough to look into his eyes.

"I believe you mean that," she said, her voice like silk wrapping around him, easing the ache in his chest.

Caleb always delivered on his commitments. He hoped like hell this time would be no different.

Chapter Five

Exhaustion dulled Katherine's senses, but she managed to follow Caleb back to the car. The visit hadn't produced any real optimism. All their hopes were riding on a dead phone.

And what if there's nothing there? a tiny voice in the back of her mind asked.

What then?

Hot, burning tears blurred Katherine's vision. Her mantra—*Chin Up. Move Forward. Forge Ahead*—had always worked. She'd survived so much of what life had thrown at her repeating those few words. Hadn't she been stronger because of it?

Then how did she explain the hollow ache in her chest? Or the niggling dread she might live out the rest of her days by herself. Everyone let her down eventually. Who could she lean on when times got tough? Who did she really have to help celebrate life's successes?

Before meeting this cowboy, she'd never realized how alone she'd truly been. She gave herself a mental shake as she opened the car door and buckled in.

Caleb found her cable-knit sweater in the back and placed it over her as she clicked the seat belt into place.

She slipped the sweater over her shoulders and closed her eyes, expecting to see the attackers' faces or to hear their threats replaying in her mind. She didn't. Instead she saw Caleb and relaxed into a deep sleep.

KATHERINE DIDN'T OPEN her eyes again until she heard Caleb's voice, raspy from lack of sleep, urging her awake. For a split second she imagined being pressed up against him, snuggled against the crook of his arm, in his big bed. She'd already been introduced, and quite intimately, to his broad chest and his long, lean, muscled thighs. He'd left no doubt he was all power, virility and man when his body had blanketed her, pinning her to the ground. Her fists had pounded pure steel abs. Warmth spread from her body to her limbs, heating her thighs.

The reality she was curled up in her car while running for Noah's life brought a slap of sanity.

"Where are we?"

"Dallas. If the address on your license is correct, we're a couple blocks from your house." He glanced at the clock. "Don't worry. We have plenty of time before the drop."

She sat up and rubbed sleep from her eyes. They were at a drive-through for a local coffee shop.

Coffee.

There couldn't be much better at the moment than a good cup of coffee save for finding Noah and having this whole nightmare behind her.

Caleb handed her a cup and took a drink from his while he pulled out of the parking lot.

"I ordered black for you."

"Perfect." Katherine took a sip of the hot liquid. The slight burn woke her senses. A blaze of sunlight appeared from the east. "You've been driving all night. You must be exhausted."

Caleb took another sip from the plastic cup. "I'm more worried about that leg of yours. At some point, we need to take another look. Didn't want to disturb you last night while you looked so peaceful."

"I'm surprised I slept at all." Katherine stretched and yawned. She glanced down at her injuries. Blood had soaked through a few of the bandages and dried. Most were intact and clear. All things considered, they were holding up. "You dressed these well. My ankle feels better already."

She touched one, then two bandages. "I think

they'll hold awhile longer. At least the bleeding has stopped."

"That's the best news I've heard all day." He cracked a sexy little smile and winked. "We'd better park here." He cut the engine. "We'll walk the rest of the way."

"Do you think they're watching my apartment?"

"A precaution," he reassured her. His clenched jaw belied his words.

"Why didn't they stop us last night? They could've waited at Leann's and shot us right then."

"I thought about that a lot on the drive. They want you to find what we're looking for. And fast."

"I didn't say anything about the file on the last call. I was too focused on Noah. They must realize I don't have it." She glanced toward her purse where the cell phone had been stashed.

"Stores don't open until ten o'clock. We have to wait to find a charging cable until then." He took a sip of coffee. "I'm guessing Noah's breathing problems must've forced them to ask for a meeting before they were ready. I think they'd rather let you locate the evidence, and then snatch you. Once they're convinced you have it, I have no doubt the game will change."

He watched over their shoulders a few times too many for Katherine's comfort, as they did their best to blend with pedestrians.

"Wait here while I scout the area." They were a few hundred feet from the front door of her apartment. He pointed toward the row of blooming crepe myrtles. There hadn't been a cold snap yet to kill the flowers. Fall weather didn't come to Dallas until mid-November some years. This was no exception.

"Okay."

A few minutes later he returned. "Looks fine from what I can tell. If they're watching, they're doing a good job of hiding. Either way, keep close to me."

She had no intention of doing anything else as she unlocked the door and followed him inside. "I wish we knew what kind of file we were looking for."

Her office had been temporarily set up in the dining room so Noah could occupy the study. From where she stood, she could see they'd taken her computer. "First Leann's laptop is missing. Now my computer. I'm guessing we're looking for a zip drive or other storage device."

"If it wasn't at your sister's place and it's not here, where else could the file be?"

"I work from home, so there's no office to go to. All I need to schedule appointments for my trainers is a computer and a phone. I keep everything here. I'll check the study where Noah's been sleeping. You might be right about Leann slipping it into his things." Katherine moved to the study that had been overtaken by her nephew. Toys spilled onto the floor. She stepped over them and rummaged through his things. No red flags were raised.

This approach wasn't working. If she were going to get anywhere, she had to figure out a way to think like Leann. Where would she stick something so incredibly valuable? Maybe Noah's suitcase? She could have removed part of the lining and tucked a file inside.

Katherine dug around until she located the small Spider-Man suitcase Noah had had in his hand when she'd met up with them. That and the rabbit he'd tucked under his arm were all the possessions he'd brought.

The Spider-Man suitcase had several pockets with zippers. Katherine checked them first. Empty. The lining was a bit more difficult to rip open but she managed without calling for help. *Sorry, buddy.* She hated to destroy his favorite bag.

Nothing there, either. Katherine tore apart the seams.

Zero.

The clock ticked. The men would expect her to produce the file soon. She had nothing to give them and still no idea what it was she was looking for. Damn.

When she returned to the living room, Caleb stood sentinel.

"No luck," she said. "She might've sent it over email."

Katherine dug around in the back of her coat closet to find her old laptop. She held it up. "This might still work."

"Your sister brought Noah to you. He was the person she most prized. Have you thought she might not have involved you because she was trying to shelter you both?"

Katherine hadn't considered Leann might be protecting her. It softened the blow. "We'll see."

A soft knock at the door kicked up Katherine's pulse.

Caleb checked through the peephole. His expression darkened. His brow arched. "Gray-haired woman. Looks to be in her mid-sixties, carrying a white puff ball."

"Does she look angry?"

"More like sour."

"Annabelle Ranker. She's my landlady, and that's her dog, Max. Big bark, no bite for the both of them." Katherine got to her feet and his strong arm was around her before she could ask for help to walk.

Caleb cracked the door open. Ms. Ranker cocked her eyebrow and looked him up and down. An approving smile quirked the corners of her iously moved by Leann's passing. "Is he home? be happy to take him off your hands while you st that foot."

"He's napping. Tuckered out from our adventure," she said quickly. A little too quickly.

The answer seemed to appease the landlady. She nodded her understanding. "I almost forgot. A package came for you while you were out. I went ahead and signed for it since you didn't answer."

Katherine had scarcely paid attention to the FedEx envelope Ms. Ranker held in one hand. Her other arm pressed her prized six-year-old Havenese, Max, to her chest.

"For me?" Katherine asked, lowering her gaze to the fur ball on Ms. Ranker's arm. "Hey, big guy."

She patted his head, stopping short of inviting them in; Ms. Ranker's arched brow said she noticed. Last thing Katherine needed was a long conversation. Besides, she wasn't prepared to discuss her situation with anyone. Except Caleb. And she'd told him things about her relationship with her sister she'd never spoken aloud to another soul. It was probably the circumstances that had her wanting to tell him everything about her. It was as if she wanted at least one person to really know her. The feeling of danger and the very real possibility she might not be alive tomorrow played tricks on her emotions. "Who's it from?"

lips. When Caleb didn't invite her in, the skeptical glare quickly returned.

No doubt, the bandages and blood wouldn't go unnoticed. Nor would the fact Katherine was gripping her old laptop as though it was fine crystal.

"Are you all right?" Her gaze traveled to Katherine's hurt foot.

"I'm fine. Got into some trouble in the woods. Turns out I'm not a nature girl. Caleb owns a nearby ranch where we visited the pumpkin patch yesterday."

"That's right. You said you were taking Noah out of the city for the day."

"We got lost in the woods. Caleb found us and helped me home." Katherine could feel heat rising up her neck. No one would ever accuse her of being a good liar. She'd kept her story as close to the truth as she could so her whole face wouldn't turn beet-red.

Ms. Ranker seemed reassured by the answer. "I wanted to check on you and the little boy. Where's Noah?"

Katherine swallowed a sob. She couldn't afford to show any emotion or to invite unwanted questions. "I'm sorry. He couldn't sleep...nightmares. We were...playing army most of the night. I've been trying to keep him busy since his mother..." Katherine diverted her eyes.

"Such a shame." Ms. Ranker shook her head,

obviously moved by Leann's passing. "Is he home? I'd be happy to take him off your hands while you rest that foot."

"He's napping. Tuckered out from our adventure," she said quickly. A little too quickly.

The answer seemed to appease the landlady. She nodded her understanding. "I almost forgot. A package came for you while you were out. I went ahead and signed for it since you didn't answer."

Katherine had scarcely paid attention to the FedEx envelope Ms. Ranker held in one hand. Her other arm pressed her prized six-year-old Havenese, Max, to her chest.

"For me?" Katherine asked, lowering her gaze to the fur ball on Ms. Ranker's arm. "Hey, big guy."

She patted his head, stopping short of inviting them in; Ms. Ranker's arched brow said she noticed. Last thing Katherine needed was a long conversation. Besides, she wasn't prepared to discuss her situation with anyone. Except Caleb. And she'd told him things about her relationship with her sister she'd never spoken aloud to another soul. It was probably the circumstances that had her wanting to tell him everything about her. It was as if she wanted at least one person to really know her. The feeling of danger and the very real possibility she might not be alive tomorrow played tricks on her emotions. "Who's it from?"

The well-meaning Ms. Ranker held out the envelope. No doubt she wanted to know more about the handsome cowboy. Plus, it wasn't like Katherine not to invite her landlady inside or to be so cryptic.

She cleared her throat and tugged at the envelope.

A slight smile was all she could expect by way of apology as the older woman loosened her grip enough for her to take possession.

Katherine's gaze flew from the return address to Caleb. The letter was from Leann. Katherine pressed it against the laptop she was still clutching.

Out of the corner of her eye, she saw the door across the courtyard open. A long metal barrel poked out. A gun?

A shower of bullets descended around them at the same time Katherine opened her mouth to warn them. A bullet slammed into the laptop. Before she could think or move, she felt the impact against her chest.

Ms. Ranker's eyes bulged before she slumped to the ground.

In the next second Caleb was on top of Katherine, covering her, protecting her.

"Are you hit?" he asked.

"I don't think so. Can't say the same for my computer." She'd dropped it the moment a bullet hit and then embedded. The hunk of metal she'd clasped to her chest had just saved her life.

He angled his head toward the kitchen. "Go. I'll fire when they get close enough."

Before she could respond, he'd urged her to keep moving as he pulled the gun to his shoulder.

When bullets exploded from the end of it, her heart hammered her chest.

Didn't matter. No time to look back. If Caleb thought she'd get out through the side window, she was in no position to argue. She clawed her way across the taupe carpet until she reached the cold tiles of the kitchen.

A moment later he was lifting her through the opened window and she was running.

Her heartbeat painfully stabbed her ribs.

Why were they shooting? They must've been watching the whole time. Did they think she'd found what they were looking for?

Oh. God. Noah. What would happen to him?

Her legs moved fast. She barely acknowledged the blood soaking her bandages. She had to run. Get out of there.

Caleb guided her to the sedan. "Get in and stay down."

Katherine curled up in a ball on the floorboard. If the bad guys knew where she lived, wouldn't they recognize her car, too?

What about Ms. Ranker? Katherine had been so

busy ducking she didn't even look. "Is my land-lady…?" Katherine couldn't finish the sentence.

Caleb shook his head. "I'm sorry."

"Max?"

"I think he got away."

Katherine gripped the envelope, fighting against the tears threatening to overwhelm her. Release the deluge and she wouldn't be able to stop. "Maybe this is what they're looking for." She held up the envelope that had cost Ms. Ranker's life.

His focus shifted from the rearview to the side mirrors. "Might be."

She ripped open the letter and overturned it on the seat.

A CD fell out.

"A file?"

"Sure looks like it." Caleb glanced around. "Stay here and stay low. Do not look up until I get back."

Before she could ask why or argue, he disappeared.

Katherine made herself into the smallest ball she could, praying for his safe return.

She couldn't even think of doing any of this without him. And yet, didn't everyone flake out on her eventually?

Even her parents.

The memory of standing on stage, alone, her senior year of high school pushed through her thoughts. The anticipation of seeing her parents' smiling faces in the crowd as she'd competed in the academic fair filled her. She'd worked hard all year and qualified with the best score her school had ever received. She'd sacrificed dates and socials to stay home and work quiz after quiz. On stage, her pulse had raced and she'd felt tiny beads of sweat trickling down her neck. She remembered thinking that if she could just see someone familiar, she'd be okay.

The curtain had opened and she'd scanned the crowd.

No one.

Disappointment and fear had gripped her. Panic had made the air thin. She'd struggled to breathe.

By the third round, she'd choked and given the wrong answer.

When she'd arrived home that evening, her parents had told her how sorry they were. They'd come home from work, opened a bottle of wine, turned on the TV and forgotten. Again.

Katherine had worked to suppress the memory from then on. She'd learned another important lesson that day. If she was going to get anywhere in life, she had only herself to depend on.

Her heart squeezed when she heard quick footsteps hustling toward her. She held her breath until Caleb's face came into view. He slipped into the driver's seat and handed over Max, his white coat splattered with red dots. He was whimpering and shaking. "Is he hurt?"

"No." Caleb turned the key in the ignition and pressed the gas. "Just scared."

Was Max covered in his owner's blood?

Katherine looked to Caleb. He dropped his right hand to his side. It was covered in blood.

"You're shot?"

"JUST A FLESH wound. Bullet grazed my shoulder. I'll be fine." Caleb hoped what he said was true. Based on the amount of blood he was losing, he couldn't be certain. He wouldn't tell Katherine though. Didn't need her to panic.

She made a move to get up, and winced.

"I'll pull over in a minute and examine us both."

Caleb glanced through his rearview, checking traffic behind them. The usual mix of sport utilities, Ford F-150s and luxury sedans sped down the North Dallas tollway.

His cell vibrated. He instructed Katherine to retrieve it from his pocket and put the call on speaker.

Matt didn't wait to speak. "My coverage has been spotty. I tried to reach you last night but couldn't."

"Everyone all right?"

"Us? We're fine. I'm concerned as hell about you."

Caleb kept watch on the road. "So far, so good here."

"Has Katherine mentioned anything about being involved in corporate espionage?"

"Of course not. I would've told you something like that. She has no idea what they're looking for."

"I guess she wouldn't tell you," Matt said. "Especially if she's involved from the get-go."

Caleb grunted but didn't speak. He had no plans to repeat himself.

"Well, ask her. The men who showed up yesterday claimed to be government officials. They asked questions about a brown-haired woman who had been seen in the area. Said she was involved in a little family business that stole and sold corporate secrets. They'd been tracking her for days before you helped her get away."

"They knew we were there?" Caleb asked. "And I don't have to ask Katherine. You're on speaker."

The line was quiet. "No. But I'm saying—"

"I already know the answer."

"You can't ignore the possibility she's involved," Matt quickly interjected.

"She's not."

"How do you know, dammit?"

"I just do."

Matt let out a frustrated hiss and a string of cuss words Caleb heard plainly through the phone.

"You just met her yesterday, and you're willing to vouch for her already? What do you know about her? You haven't met any of her people. She could've been hurt while running from the government for all we know."

"I told you once so I won't repeat myself. What else did they say?"

"One thing is sure. She shows up then suddenly we have official-looking men coming out of the woodwork. All we have to go on is her word. She claims there was a kidnapping, but did you actually see the kid?"

No, he hadn't seen the boy. That didn't mean there wasn't one. He'd seen the pictures of him. Had been there moments after Noah had been taken. He'd seen kid toys at her sister's place and at Katherine's. Besides, Caleb had seen the sheer terror on her face. He could still see the agony in her violet eyes. This conversation was going nowhere. He needed to redirect. She most definitely did not make this up, and he hated the fact she had to hear his friend's accusations. "The kid has a name. Noah. Did you speak to Coleman?"

"Sheriff doesn't know what to believe. Said he'd follow up through proper channels to see if the men were legit, but it could take a while. He doesn't exactly have ready access to the kinds of people who can verify something like this. Those men who showed up looked serious to me. They flipped badges, too."

"Doesn't mean anything."

"That's exactly what Coleman said. They looked pretty damn official from where I stood."

"Can Coleman find out if there is a 'Kane' involved in a federal investigation?"

"He's trying but he said not to hold out a lot of hope."

"Anything else?" Caleb tensed against the pain in his shoulder.

"Take her to the nearest government building and turn her in, Caleb. Before this gets even more out of control."

"You know I won't."

"I don't think it's safe for you here at the ranch," Matt said quietly.

"I won't put my men at risk. I won't come home until this is settled."

There was a long silence.

"Then for God's sake, be careful," Matt warned.

"Got it covered."

"I'll keep things working here until you get back."

"Always knew I could count on you." The pressure in Caleb's chest eased. His men would be covered until his return.

"How's Jimmy's little girl?"

"Not good. They scheduled surgery for her in Dallas."

"They found a donor?"

"Seems like it."

"That's good news."

Jimmy's daughter would get the chance she deserved. He'd ensure Katherine did, too.

Caleb asked Katherine to end the call.

She looked at him deadpan. "Why didn't you tell me Matt thinks I'm involved?"

"He's not sure what to believe." Caleb glanced down at her. She looked helpless and small. His protective instincts flared. He wanted to guard her from Matt's accusations as much as the men chasing her. Those full cherry lips and chestnut hair stirred him sexually. Caleb would swim with caution in the emotional tide.

"What about Jimmy's daughter?"

"She was born with a bad heart. They found a donor. Her surgery is scheduled in a few days." Caleb hoped like hell he'd be around for it.

Katherine frowned. "Children should get to grow up before they have to give up their childhood. They shouldn't have to deal with sickness or death at such young ages. It seems so unfair."

"Agreed."

Her back went rigid as she took in a breath. "Okay. What's next?"

"We need to find a laptop or computer to figure out what's so important on the disk. Coleman's checking into the other. If the men who showed up turn out to be government, there could be anything on that CD."

"And now you don't believe me, either?"

"When did I say that?"

Katherine set the CD down on the seat next to Max. Anger and resentment scored her normally soft features. "You didn't have to. I was putting myself in your shoes."

"Don't."

"What if they do work for the government but whoever's behind this is paying them off?"

"There could be one bad egg. Not this many. Besides, Coleman doesn't think they're legit. He's expecting to find ghosts as he investigates. We can give him a call."

"Would he sit on this kind of information?"

"No. He'd contact me right away."

"Whatever's on this CD caused my nephew to be kidnapped. I want to find the bastard who did this and make him pay. He deserves to be in jail."

"You're right." Caleb pulled over, and then concentrated on his phone. The map feature produced three coffee shops and an internet café nearby. "There's a place a few blocks from here we might be able to go into."

He'd have a chance to inspect their injuries. Caleb's shirtsleeve was soaked. He needed to stop the bleeding.

Chapter Six

Katherine fumbled for her cell as it buzzed for the second time. The screen read Private.

Caleb parked the car in a crowded lot as she answered before the call transferred to voice mail, hoping she might recognize the voice if she heard it again.

"Did you find what you've been looking for?" His tone was smooth and practiced, and she detected a slight accent. His cool and calm demeanor made the hairs on the back of her neck prickle.

Frustration got the best of her. "What do you think you'll accomplish by hurting me? Not to mention the fact I can't find anything for you if I'm dead. You didn't have to kill an innocent person to get what you want. I'll gladly give it to you when I find it." Could she ask about the government men without giving Caleb away?

"Are you saying you don't have the file?" the even voice said.

"That's not answering my question. Who were those men you sent to kill me?"

"Let's just say I have very loyal employees."

Damn him for being so composed when her world had crumbled around her. She gripped her sister's CD tighter. Anything could be on there. She hoped this was the file they wanted, but she couldn't be sure. Besides, if she said yes and was wrong, she'd be signing a death warrant for Noah. She had to stall them. "Tell me what I'm looking for. I want to help you. I want Noah back and I want this nightmare over."

"What was in the envelope?"

"I don't know what you're talking about." Fire crawled up her neck at the lie. If he could see her now, she'd be exposed.

"Don't play games with me." Anger cracked his voice.

"At least give me a hint. There's a world of possibilities and I have to get this right." Panic made her hands shake. *Breathe.*

Caleb covered her hand with his. His touch calmed her rising pulse.

"Your sister knew exactly what I was talking about. My bet is you do, too."

"Is that why you tried to kill me?" Katherine railed against the urge to scream. She suppressed her need to tell him what he could do with his file. She had to think about Noah. Nothing mattered more than bringing him home safely. "I'm afraid I'm at a disadvantage here. My sister and I weren't that close. She didn't tell me much of anything. Just used me as a free babysitter." Katherine hated playing nice with this guy when she wanted to climb through the phone connection and do horrible things to him. "How's my nephew?"

"Not good if you don't get me what I want."

Katherine's heart pummeled her ribs. "How's his breathing?"

"I won't let anything happen to him. Not unless you don't cooperate."

"Let me speak to him. I won't do anything else until I know he's okay. You won't like it if I disappear," she hedged.

The phone went silent. *Damn.* Anger them more and Noah could pay the ultimate price. She struggled to hold back the tears that were threatening. Let one drop and the avalanche would come.

"Auntie?" His voice sounded small and frail, nothing like his usual boisterous self.

Her heart skipped. "Noah. Baby, listen to me. Everything's going to be okay." He couldn't panic. Not with his condition. "We're going to get your medicine."

"I don't like it here." His sniffles punctured her heart.

"They didn't hurt you, did they?" She struggled to keep her voice calm.

"No. They're nice."

"I need you to be very brave. Can you do that?"

"Uh-huh."

"Be good. Listen to what they say. I promise I'm coming to get you as soon as I can."

Before he could respond, a shuffling noise came through the static on the line.

"Bring the file to the drop alone if you ever want to see him alive again."

Click.

Katherine stared out the window as Max wriggled in her lap.

Caleb took the phone from her and placed it on the console between them. "We'll get him back. He's okay. That's the most important thing right now."

"Why would they call again?"

Caleb shrugged. "Insurance."

"Hearing him…knowing how frightened he is… how brave he's being…" She took a deep breath. "It pains me to sit by like this and feel like I'm doing nothing."

"I understand. He's showing real courage. He got that from you." His words caressed her tired heart. Brought it back to life so that it beat again without painful stabs.

Katherine wanted to cry. To release all the pent-up frustration, anger and worry she'd been holding in throughout this ordeal. *And during her entire life,* she thought as she realized she hadn't really cried in more years than she could count. She'd trained herself to sidestep her emotions after her parents died. She'd needed to be the strong one.

At first, she had tried to reach out for help.

Anthony, her first love, had promised to visit every month after she'd had to leave school to go home and care for her sister. His calls were her saving grace. The two jobs she'd worked were barely enough to keep them fed. It was even harder to keep her grades up when she'd lived on little more than a few hours of sleep. But she'd done it. She'd kept her head above water.

His voice, the eye in the storm, had become her lifeline. Without him, she'd feared everything that was still *her* would wash away in the tide and she'd never be the same person again.

With every reassurance he'd given, her confidence had grown. She could do it. She could make it work. She could take care of her sister and still have something of a life left.

Then the calls stemmed. Excuses about conflicting schedules came. And, eventually, the phone stopped ringing.

She'd learned through the grapevine that he'd been dating someone else.

She'd been devastated.

When she'd needed him the most to lean on, he wasn't there, but she had learned from it. Learned to rely on herself and not to depend on others. Learned that other people were disappointments. Learned to keep her walls high and march on. But had she built walls so high no one could penetrate them?

The men she'd dated since had spent more time at sporting events than with her, and she was fine with it.

Outside the window, the rain started coming down. Big drops fell, making large splotches on the windshield.

"I couldn't put my finger on it before. There's something different about the way the guy speaks. You heard him before when we listened to his message on speaker at your house."

"I don't remember an accent."

"Only certain words." She turned to meet Caleb's gaze, and a well of need sprung inside her.

He stroked the back of her neck, pulling her lips closer to his. He was so strong. Capable.

His dark eyes closed the moment his lips pressed to hers, and she surrendered to the kiss. Completely. Freely. With a need burning so brightly inside her, the flames almost engulfed her.

His tongue pulsed inside her mouth and fire shot straight to the insides of her thighs. How could she want a man so instantly? So absolutely? So thoroughly? Her nipples heightened to pointed peaks, straining for his touch. *More.* She wanted all of him, which was even more reason getting involved with him further would be a bad idea.

Katherine pulled back. "You're hurt. We should check out your injury."

"It's a scratch," he said dismissively, his low gravelly baritone sending another round of sensitized shivers skittering across her nerves.

A pained expression crossed his features, and Katherine knew it was more than from his shoulder. She looked into his gaze and saw something reckless...dangerous...sexy.

Wouldn't he leave when this was all over?

She refused to invest in another relationship, because they didn't work. She'd wind up hurt, and she didn't have it inside her to go through that pain again.

"Let's check it out anyway. I'd feel better if I knew you were going to be okay."

He rolled up his sleeve, revealing a deep gash in solid muscle. He must've caught the panic in her eyes because he quickly said, "It's not as bad as it looks."

"You need to get that checked out."

"I'm not going anywhere until I see this through." His eyes locked on to her as he gripped the steering wheel. "So forget about that."

She clamped her lips shut. Hope filled her chest.

"We should find somewhere we can clean up.

I can get supplies. I'm sure people will be suspicious if we stroll into a café looking like this."

"What about the men in suits? I have no idea what my sister got involved in. I don't think she would steal anything, let alone blackmail, but I don't really know. Based on my recent conversation, I think there's some kind of corporation involved."

Caleb started the engine. "We'll get cleaned up and check the CD first." He played around on his phone before putting the gearshift into Drive. "We might have everything we're looking for in our hands already."

He blended into traffic at the next light.

"Whoever those men are, they aren't here to help. They kidnapped your nephew. Tried to take you, too. They've fired at us in broad daylight. They knew where we were, so they've been following us or someone was waiting, watching your place." He issued a grunt. "It'd take one big secret to bring on what we faced today."

"Or one powerful man."

"Your sister made a big enemy out of someone important. The question is who has this much influence? This Kane guy?"

"I have no idea. It'd have to be someone who has the ability to make permanent accidents happen. Send men at a moment's notice to erase people."

Caleb nodded. "Everything's online now. If we

had her computer, we might be able to find an electronic trail."

"I'm scared." The admission came when she least expected to voice it.

"I won't let anything happen to you." Even though the set of his jaw said he meant every one of those words, he couldn't guarantee them.

Katherine didn't respond. What could she say?

"The biggest thing he has going for him is that we don't know who he is. I wish there was some way to flush him out."

"I hope we have everything we need in here to find him." The information she needed *had* to be on that CD or Leann's phone. Anything else was unthinkable.

Caleb parked in front of a hotel and excused himself, returning a few minutes later holding a card key. "Once we clean ourselves up and get supplies, we'll check out that disk. Tuck Max into your sweater."

She hobbled out of the sedan. Her stomach growled, reminding her how long it had been since she'd last eaten. It didn't matter. Food wouldn't go down on her queasy stomach. Her nerves would be fried until she knew what was on that CD.

The room was simple and tasteful. The dark wood furniture was modern with clean lines. Artistically angled framed photos of flowers hung above the king-size bed. There was a desk with chair, a minifridge and microwave.

The card on the bed said it was "Heavenly." Katherine didn't need a note to tell her the fluffy white blanket would feel amazing wrapped around her. Add Caleb's arms to the mix and she could sleep for days in his embrace. She quickly canceled the thought. Didn't need to go there again with thoughts of what Caleb could do for her on a bed.

He held up a towel. "Why don't you clean up first?"

"Okay."

"Do you need help?"

She set Max down. Caleb poured water into a coffee cup and placed it on the floor for the little dog to drink.

"I can handle it," Katherine said as she closed the bathroom door behind her.

"Take care with those cuts. I'll clean Max before I head out to pick up supplies. With any luck, I'll find a charger while I'm out." His voice was so close she could tell he'd stopped at the door. "Keep that foot elevated."

Katherine glanced down at her leg. If she looked anything on the outside like she felt on the inside, she dreaded looking into a mirror. Freshening up suddenly sounded like a good idea.

CALEB RETURNED HALF an hour later with bags of food and supplies. "I found a big-box store and picked up antibiotic ointment and gauze. I located a battery for the cell phone, too. I popped the CD into one of their laptops. Nothing unusual jumped out at me. All I saw were pictures of Noah."

Her violet eyes went wide. "That's it?"

"Maybe we'll find more when we go downstairs to the business center and have more time to look."

She nodded.

"As for the cell, I found an interesting number. Did she ever talk about Bolden Holdings?"

"No."

"Sebastian Kane's the CEO. I don't know why I didn't connect the dots sooner. I've seen him on the cover of *Forbes* before. Any chance that accent you picked up on is Canadian?"

Her head rocked back and forth. "Very well could be. But why would my sister be involved with him? Seriously? What issue could a man like that possibly have with her? How could she have information about his company?"

"Someone like Kane would care about money and his reputation. I'm betting she somehow got tangled up with him. She could've been dating him. We don't know anything for sure. Maybe that CD will tell us specifically. Maybe there's a picture of them together. I sent a text to Coleman. He's following the lead."

"Before we go downstairs, I should check your shoulder."

"After I take care of your ankle," he insisted. "But first, I've been thinking. Could your sister have had a job you didn't know about? Did she ever talk about her work?"

"She had a part-time job as a barista at Coffee Hut. Said it allowed her to go in early in the morning before Noah was awake. The neighbor sat with him. Then she could take late-morning classes and still be home for him after lunch."

Didn't sound like the kind of person who would go rogue and steal much of anything. Let alone someone who would have the guts to blackmail a major player. Then again, her money was tight. She might have risked it all to be able to spend more time with her son. "I know she didn't mention the father to you, but what kind of guys did she normally date?"

A throaty laugh came from Katherine. "Before Noah? Every kind. She dated smart guys. Athletes. Ones who grew their hair long and ate nothing but kale. I don't think she was seeing anyone lately. She calmed down considerably since she had a baby. Said she couldn't remember the last time she'd had sex."

A blush reddened her cheeks at the admission.

Caleb could feel his heartbeat at the base of his throat. She was sexy when she was embarrassed.

Caleb motioned for her to sit on the bed while he positioned the desk chair in front of her and sat on the edge.

"You think she got mixed up dating Kane? Maybe saw something or found something while she was at his place?"

"Anything's possible. Hard to imagine her in a relationship with the head of a conglomerate. Although, she was beautiful."

"She could've met him at work. Maybe he stopped into the coffee shop where she worked? We could find a way to ask her coworkers."

Katherine had cleaned up and looked even more sexy wrapped in a bath towel. The thought of her naked in the shower sent heat rocketing through him. That was the last thing he *should* be thinking about. But hell, if he were being honest, he'd admit seeing her naked was actually at the top of his list of appealing ideas. He gave in to his appreciation for her body. Looking at those long, lean legs, small waist and smooth hips stirred an immediate reaction. When his gaze slid from the smooth curve of her calves down her slender ankles to her bare feet, his mouth dried.

He forced his gaze to her face.

She slicked her tongue over her lips and damned if the image wasn't even sexier. He lowered his gaze to her neck. Her chest rose and fell with her rapid breathing. He saw her breasts tighten under the thin fabric of the towel.

The need to protect her and kiss her surged. If he didn't get a grip she'd know exactly how badly he wanted to make love to her.

Max's bark crashed him back to reality.

He forced himself to think rationally. She was in trouble. He was there to help.

He'd have to work harder to contain his growing attraction.

"Let's get a look at those." He hated the idea of causing her more pain, but her cuts needed tending to, and she needed antibiotic ointment. He'd have to get her to a clinic soon for a tetanus shot, too.

"What about your injuries? We should make sure you're okay," she said, her lips set in a frown.

"I'll live. Do you always put others first?" He wasn't used to that. Wasn't he always the one saving the day? Rescuing others? Denying himself?

"What if something happens to you? Is there anyone I should notify? Girlfriend?"

"Not now. A few before."

She gifted him with her first real smile of the day.

"I told myself I didn't have time for them when I moved into the Dust Bowl Ranch outside San Antonio as a kid. I was busy working and trying to stay under the radar."

"I'm sure they made time for you."

He shrugged. "I dated around. Couldn't find anyone special enough to marry." Caleb figured he'd rather spend his time building his empire than on an evening out with a woman who made him want to stick toothpicks in his eyes for how dull the conversation was. Waiting for the right girl had taken too long. He'd dated here and there. He'd all but given up when Cissy showed up. "Almost got married once."

"What happened?"

"Didn't work out. She left. Said life on the ranch was boring." He didn't want to get into the details about the little girl she'd taken with her. Savannah had been all smiles and freckles. Her heart was bigger than the land. Caleb still wondered if Cissy was taking good enough care of the little angel.

"How long ago was that?"

"Couple of months, I guess." Caleb tucked the remaining gauze back into the box and closed the lid. "Leg's looking better. Swelling's going down. I thought it might get worse after all the running today. Take these." He handed her a couple of ibuprofen and a bottle of water.

"Not sure if I'll know what to do without pain," she said with a weak smile.

He liked that she was relaxing with him. Her sticking around was an idea he could get used to. He mentally slapped himself. Nothing personal, but the last thing Caleb needed to do was to get romantically involved with another woman who needed rescuing. Even if this did feel...different.

Keeping his feelings in check became a bigger priority. Besides, they needed to get dressed and find the business center.

"Took a guess at your size." He tossed the bag onto the bed. "Think you'll find a few things in there you can wear. Can't promise they'll be fashionable."

Katherine took out the cotton shorts and pink T-shirt, blushing at the underwear and bra. "These will work fine."

Caleb fed Max, and then moved to the sink in the bathroom. He unbuttoned his shirt and shrugged it off.

In the mirror, he saw Katherine, now dressed, approaching. She stopped when she saw his shirt was off. Her gaze drifted across his bare torso.

A lightning bolt of heat spread through him, flowing blood south.

Not one woman had brought instant lust like this before. The closest he'd ever been to this was with Michelle and that still paled in comparison. She'd appeared at his doorway broke, asking for work. She'd had no money and no place to live.

He'd taken her in and helped her find a job. It hadn't taken her long to figure out where his bedroom was.

The sex had been hot. Chemistry outside the bedroom, not.

She'd moved her things in though, and seemed intent on staying for a while.

Caleb had started working longer hours than usual, looking for excuses to stay out of the house. Eventually, she'd left. No note.

He'd learned his lesson. He didn't do sex for sex's sake anymore.

Sex with Katherine would be amazing. No, mind-blowing. He had no doubt they'd sizzle with chemistry under the sheets.

Connecting in the everyday world would be no different than his past relationships. At least that's what he told himself. The thought this could be anything deeper or more real scared the hell out of him.

Katherine cleared her throat. "Here. Let me help you with that."

She moved next to him without making eye contact, took a clean washcloth from the counter, rinsed it under the tap and wrung it out. Dabbing his gash, she pressed her silken fingers to his shoulder. Contact sent his hormones into overdrive. Need for her surged faster than he could restrain. His erection pulsed, reminding him of all the things he'd like to do to her and with her. He wanted to be inside her. Now.

"Get ready. This might hurt," she said with a tentative smile, scooting in front of him.

"I'm fine." But was he? His head might be screwed on straight, but his body had ideas of the sexual variety. Damned if he wasn't thinking about sex with Katherine again.

She rubbed the wound with the washcloth until it was clean. Next, she gently dabbed antibiotic ointment on the cut.

He wasn't used to hands like hers. Soft and tender. It felt like a caress.

A crack appeared in his mind, like light in a small dark tunnel. His exterior armor threatened to splinter. He couldn't figure out why he'd told Katherine about Cissy. Weren't those wounds still fresh? Didn't they sting worse than the exterior cut on his shoulder?

Shouldn't he feel guilty for being this close to a woman in a hotel room given that Cissy had walked out so recently?

He didn't.

Instead he felt the strange sensation of warmth and light that accompanied allowing someone to take care of him for a change.

The whole concept was foreign to him. He'd taken care of himself and everyone around him for as long as he could remember.

Her touch, the way it seemed so natural to have her hands on him, suddenly felt more dangerous than the men with guns. All they could do was end a person's life. A woman like Katherine could make it not worth living without her.

Caleb eradicated the thought.

She was a woman in trouble. He was there to help. When this was all over, she'd go back to her life and he'd return to his.

He backed away and slipped on a new T-shirt. "Let's see about that CD."

Chapter Seven

Katherine tucked Max inside her handbag and followed Caleb downstairs. The business center was a small room adjacent to the lobby. A wall of desks and two computers occupied the space. The wall between the business center and the lobby was made of glass. There wasn't much in the way of privacy, but it would have to do.

Katherine fished the CD out of her bag and handed it to Caleb.

Max squirmed and whimpered.

"Poor little guy. You miss her, don't you?" A wave of melancholy flooded Katherine as she stroked his fur. "He lost his home."

"He can come to the ranch. Unless you want him."

"Might be too sad to go home with me. Although when this ordeal is settled, I'll be looking for a new place to live. Can't imagine going back to my apartment after…"

"Either way, he'll have a new home."

"Poor little guy might need to go out soon after eating and drinking all that water."

"I saw a green space on the side of the building. We can take him there as soon as we see what we're dealing with here."

There was one file on the disk. It was labeled "Katherine."

Caleb's gaze flicked from hers to the computer screen. "Nothing stood out before. Let's see if a closer look tells us what your sister wanted you to know."

Katherine's pulse raced. She took a deep breath. "Okay."

He clicked on her name as she looked over his shoulder.

"I can't help but wonder why she would send snapshots of Noah through FedEx when she was meeting me to hand him off."

"She must've realized she was being followed and wanted to be sure they weren't intercepted. Let's look through 'em. See if we can find a clue." Caleb started the slide show.

Katherine watched, perplexed, as picture after picture of Noah filled the screen. There were photographs of him at Barton Creek. He'd been to the zoo. It looked like a montage of his summer activities.

"Check your email. It's possible she sent you a note. Pull up her last few messages and look for anything that might signal the file's whereabouts. There might be hints. A word out of place in a sentence. A location she mentions more than once. See if there's anything we can go on."

She logged on remotely. There was nothing unusual as she scanned the last couple of notes from Leann. No extra emails from her sister mysteriously appearing posthumously, either. Not a single clue.

From the lobby, the TV volume cranked up.

"An elderly woman has been gunned down in front of her neighbor's apartment in a normally quiet suburb. The news has rocked a small North Dallas community. The name of the deceased is being withheld until family can be notified but two persons of interest, Katherine Harper and an unidentified male, are believed to have information that would assist in the investigation. An eyewitness saw them running from the scene with a weapon, and police are warning citizens not to approach them but to call 9-1-1 if they are spotted..."

Katherine's heart dropped. She glanced around. The man behind the registration desk picked up the phone and stared at her. Was he phoning the police? She nudged Caleb.

He turned around and cursed under his breath. "How on earth could we be tied to Ms. Ranker's murder?" The feeling of being trapped made her pulse climb. How would they get out of the hotel unseen? And if they did, where would they go? Everyone in the area would be looking for them. If they so much as tried to get coffee or food, they might be spotted. There would be nowhere to hide.

Caleb ejected the CD. "We'll figure this out later. Right now, we've gotta get out of here."

"Do we have time to get back to the room? I left everything in there but my purse and Max."

"I don't know how much time we have, but we need to try. I changed clothes and the car keys are in my old pants."

An uninvited image of Caleb's shirtless chest invaded Katherine's thoughts. Reality crashed fast and hard. She glanced around wildly as Caleb led her out of the business center half afraid the guy working the front desk would give chase.

As soon as they entered the stairwell, he urged her to run. They made it up the couple flights of stairs easily thanks to the ibuprofen tablets she'd taken earlier. The medicine saved her from the pain that would be shooting up her leg otherwise.

Caleb stopped at the door. "I'll grab everything I can. You watch the hall. If anyone darkens that corridor, let me know. A second's notice might be the difference between freedom and jail."

He disappeared.

Not a minute later, the elevator dinged.

Katherine stepped inside the room. "Someone's coming."

"Damn." He threw a bag of supplies over his shoulder and took her hand. His grip was firm as he broke into a full run, leading her to the opposite stairwell.

"Stop!" came from behind.

Katherine glanced back. A man dressed in a suit and wearing dark glasses gave chase. How could they escape? Where would they go?

She and Caleb slipped inside the stairwell. The shuffle of feet coming toward them sounded at the same time Max whimpered. How would they get anywhere quietly with him on board?

"It's okay, boy," she whispered. His big dark eyes looked up at her from the bag, and she realized the little guy was shaking. Max was in a totally foreign environment without his owner. *Poor thing.* She lifted him and cradled him to her chest to calm him.

The door from the third floor smacked against the wall at almost the same time as the one from the floor below them. With men coming in both directions, they were sandwiched with no way out.

"Stick close to me," Caleb said, squeezing her hand.

He entered the second floor.

Halfway down the hall, the maid's cart framed a door.

"In here," he said, urging her toward it.

"We'll be cornered in there. I don't see another way out."

"Trust me." Caleb darted toward the room as he glanced back.

She saw more than a hint of recklessness in his eyes now—a throwback to his misspent youth? "How did you get so good at evading people?"

"I told you, I had a rough childhood. Learned a lot of things I didn't want to need to know as an adult." Caleb ducked into the room and shooed out the cleaning lady as doors opened from both ends of the hallway. He slid the dead bolt into place.

Shots were fired and Katherine ducked. Oh. God. She was going to die right there.

Before she could scream, Caleb pulled her to the floor and covered her with his body. His broad, masculine chest flush with her back, she felt the steady rhythm of his heartbeat.

More shots were fired; bullets pinged through the walls. She had the split-second fear her life was about to end and all she could think about was her family. The memories brought a melancholy mix of pain and happiness coursing through her.

What did Caleb have?

Other than his mother, hadn't he been alone most

of his life? Her heart ached for him. Maybe that's why he'd gotten so good at taking care of others.

Because of her, he'd end up in jail or dead today.

His exterior was tough. Tall, with dark brown eyes she could look into for days. With his broad shoulders, lean hips, stacked muscles, he was physical strength personified. His substantial presence would affect anyone. He was like steel. But what did he have to fortify from within?

Katherine felt herself being pulled to her feet as she held tight to Max. He'd stopped whimpering. "What are we doing?"

He made quick work jimmying the window open. "Escaping."

A bullet pinged near Katherine's head. Caleb pulled her to the floor and covered her again before she had a chance to react.

The bullets stopped as a thump sounded against the door. Could they kick it in?

"From here on out, we've got to stay off the grid." His carved-from-granite features were stone.

Katherine took a moment to absorb his words. He was saying they couldn't show their faces again in public. They'd go into hiding and then what? How would they eat? And worse yet, what would happen to Noah? How would she make it to the drop? The center of a mall was about as public of a place as she could imagine.

The crack of an object slamming into the door wrenched her from her shock.

"You climb out first. I'll hold you as long as I can." He set Max on the floor. "I'll toss him down to you, and then I want you to run. Don't wait for me. You hear?"

Not wait for him? Was he kidding? Katherine wouldn't make it two steps without Caleb.

"But—"

"No time."

She sat on the edge of the window for a second to gather her nerves. Caleb helped her twist onto her belly to ease the impact to her leg. He lowered her.

"Ready?"

She nodded, bracing for the impact on her hurt leg. She landed hard. Her legs gave out. As soon as she turned, Caleb was half hanging out the window, making himself as low to the ground as he could before he made sure she was ready and then he let Max drop.

Catching him with both hands, she breathed a sigh of relief when Caleb followed almost immediately after.

"Aren't we near Mockingbird and 75?" he asked as he broke into a run.

"Yeah, but my car's the other direction." Katherine pointed west.

"We have a better shot of getting lost if we can get to the train."

Then what?

Before Katherine could wind up a good anxiety attack, a flurry of men in dark suits came pouring out of the building.

She powered her legs forward to the edge of the lot with the adrenaline thumping through her, ignoring the throbbing pain coursing up her leg. Caleb pushed them forward until they disappeared into a tree line.

The roar of the train sounded nearby.

"If we can get across the tracks, we can make it." He lifted her as if she weighed nothing and sprinted toward the station.

The train was coming fast. Too fast. They'd never make it in time, especially with him carrying her. "I can run."

"Not a chance." Caleb picked up speed, clearing the rail with seconds to spare.

The train car doors opened and he hopped inside, placing Katherine in the first available seat. She prayed the Dallas Area Rapid Transit police or fare-enforcement officers wouldn't be checking passengers for tickets. The last thing they needed was to give someone a reason to notice them, and she remembered reading the rail had increased security after a series of recent murders.

She tucked Max in her purse and watched out

the window as the buildings blurred. "Think they saw us?"

"It's a pretty good bet. We'll jump off at the next stop. Get lost somewhere on the Katy Trail."

The engine slowed and the light rail train stopped. They hopped off.

She didn't want to weigh them down. His shoulder was bleeding again from carrying her. He'd never admit it, but he had to be exhausted by now. He was going on no sleep as it was. "I can make it."

"You sure?"

Katherine nodded. They ran for a few minutes before her leg gave out. "I'm sorry. I need a rest."

He found a small clearing and stopped to catch their breath. "Squeeze into these bushes. This should provide enough cover to hide us for now."

Katherine was beginning to wonder if she'd ever feel secure again.

He took Max from her arms. "Better let him stretch his legs."

Max scuttled to a nearby bush and relieved himself.

"C'mon, boy," Caleb said, patting his leg. His breathing was hardly accelerated whereas Katherine's lungs burned.

The sound of pounding footsteps broke the quiet.

Peering through the leaves, Katherine's heart

skittered when she saw the men in suits. They were staring at something in their hands.

Caleb backed out of the underbrush and urged her on the move again as he scooped up Max.

The men seemed to be a few feet behind everywhere they went.

"It's no use," she said, panting. The pain in her leg was staggering.

"Dammit. I didn't even think about this before. It makes sense now."

"What are you talking about?"

"Give me your phone." He held out his free hand.

She dug it out of her purse and placed it on his flat palm.

"Hold Max."

She did.

He pulled out the battery and smashed the phone under the heel of his cowboy boot. Did the same to his own. Then picked up the pieces and tossed them.

Panic gripped her as it felt like icy fingers had closed around her chest and squeezed. All the air sucked out of her lungs in a whooshing sound. "They can't contact me now. What have you done?"

"They can't find us anymore, either." He took her hand in his. "They've been following us using the GPS tracking in the phone. It's the only way they could always be a step behind."

"How can they do that unless they work for the government?"

"It's surprisingly easy. Anyone can buy the program online." He urged her forward as he took Max, and then ran for what seemed like half an hour before stopping. "We should be safe now."

She hobbled a few feet and settled onto a large rock, stroking Max and fighting waves of tears from exhaustion and panic. "Any idea where we are?"

Caleb shook his head.

He sat beside her and braided their fingers together. "You don't have to keep it together all the time."

Yes, she did. He didn't understand. She had to be strong for Noah. She'd had to be strong her entire life. "I have a lot of responsibility, and the last thing I can afford to do is break down." She sniffed back a tear.

"It's okay to cry. I'm right here, and I'm not going anywhere."

Her heart skipped a beat when she realized those words comforted her far more than she should allow. She shivered and raised her gaze to meet his. Warmth spread through her body.

His chest moved up and down rhythmically, whereas her breathing was ragged. And not just because she'd outrun bullets and scary men with guns. Her pulse rose for a different reason. His body was so close she could breathe in his masculinity. Her arms were full of goose bumps. She knew the instant her body shifted from fear to awareness...

Awareness of his strong hands on her. Awareness of the unique scent of woods and outdoors and virility that belonged to him. Awareness of everything that was Caleb. A sensual shiver raced up her spine.

Being close to him, drinking in his powerful scent was a mistake. Katherine needed a clear head. Especially because she could so vividly recall the way his lips tasted. How soft they were when they moved with hers.

Katherine's heart beat somewhere at the base of her throat, thumping wildly.

Wisps of his sandy-blond curls moved in the wind. His rich brown-gold eyes were fixed on her, blazing. In that moment she wanted nothing more than to explore the steel muscles under the cotton fabric of his T-shirt. Her hands itched to trace his jawline to the dimple in his chin.

Guilt slammed into her. How could she allow herself to become distracted? Noah was the only person who mattered. He needed her now more than ever. Nothing could ever happen between her and Caleb. *Not now. Not ever.* She had a family to think about, and a drop spot to get to. *Refocus.*

"I still can't believe my sister would have had anything to do with a man like Kane."

"I've read he has his hand on everything that crosses the borders from Canada to Mexico."

"Which makes even less sense to me. How would my sister be connected to a man like that? She didn't have any money. She worked at a coffee shop, for God's sake. I know she could keep a secret, but she didn't run in circles like that." Katherine gripped the tree branch tighter. "Wish we could've had more time to check out that CD. Maybe there's a hidden file or something? All I could see were pictures of Noah. Which would make a person think that's all she was sending, but we both know it can't be right."

"Especially when she sent them 'signature required.'" Caleb redressed one of her injuries.

"You said you got into trouble when you were young. What happened?"

He didn't look up. He put away supplies as he finished with them and rolled them into a ball, placing them in a backpack. He patted Max on the head. "I told you. I had a few run-ins with the law when I was younger. Gave my mom a hard time. Stopped when I saw what it was doing to her. End of story."

"Did you act out because of your father?"

He scratched behind Max's ears. The little dog had stopped shaking and sat at Caleb's feet.

"He'll need to eat again soon." The subject had been changed.

All she knew about the handsome cowboy was that he saved cats, dogs and women in trouble. Katherine wished he would open up more.

"You hungry, too?" His jaw did that tick thing again.

She figured the subject of his father was closed.

CALEB NEEDED TO find safe shelter for Katherine. He needed to protect her from everyone and everything bad more than he needed air. Help her, yes, but where had this burning need to banish all her pain come from? He could feel her anguish as if it were his own.

A crack of thunder in the distance threatened a storm.

By tying them to Ms. Ranker's murder, everyone would be on the lookout for him and Katherine now. No place would be safe. They were wanted. Had no transportation. If they ducked their heads inside the wrong building, they'd be shot at or captured.

The police wouldn't believe their story, so going to them was out.

He and Katherine would need to change their appearance and figure out a place to bed down tonight. But where? He could think of a dozen or so places he could hide her on the ranch.

A lone thought pounded his temples. What would Kane have to gain by getting them arrested?

Dammit. Was there a mole in the police station? A man like Kane could buy a lot of goodwill. Could he ensure they didn't make it out of jail, too?

The DART rail system could get them as far as Plano. The hike back would be dangerous. If anyone spotted them, they would most likely call 9-1-1. How much longer could they outrun a man with Kane's resources?

He had no idea how he'd survive this, let alone keep Katherine and Noah safe. That little boy deserved a life. He had a right to be loved and to have the kind of family she would provide. He deserved Katherine.

She'd be a better mother than she thought. She was risking her life for the child. That kind of dedication and love would ensure Noah had an amazing childhood.

The boy had already lost the one person he was closest to in the world. A pang of regret sliced through Caleb. He knew exactly what it was like to lose a mother. The overwhelming pain that came with realizing he was all alone in the world.

An urge to protect Noah surged so strongly inside he was completely caught off guard.

He refocused on Katherine. Watching her as she tried to be brave would wear down his resolve not to touch her. He fought like hell against the urge to take her in his arms and comfort her already. A little question mark lingered in the back of his mind. Did she want him the way he wanted her?

He could feel her body react to him every time he touched her. Yet she pulled away.

Dammit.

Under another set of circumstances, he would like to take his time to get to know her. Take her out somewhere nice for dinner. Learn about where she went to college and more about the kind of software company she worked for. Date. Like normal people.

Caleb almost laughed out loud.

His life had been anything but *normal*. And this impossible situation was only getting worse. The more time he spent with her, the louder his danger alarms sounded. She was already under his skin, and he wanted to get closer.

His biggest fear was that he wouldn't be able to protect her when the time came, and he would lose her forever. They'd narrowly escaped several times in the past few hours.

Her resolve was weakening.

He could go a few more days without sleep, and his only injury came from his shoulder. He could fix it with a sterile needle and thread. Neither of those was on him at present. He was running out of options for places to hide.

He'd take her to the only place he'd ever truly felt safe, his ranch…and figure out a way to get a message to Matt. Then he'd have to find a way to keep his family safe.

Chapter Eight

Katherine's chestnut hair had been pulled up loosely in a ponytail. Caleb's fingers itched from wanting to feel the stray strands that framed her face. The desire to reach out, touch her, be her comfort, was an ache in his chest. But he couldn't be her shelter now and still walk away later when this whole ordeal had passed. No use putting much stock in the emotions occupying his thoughts. He checked the area and deemed it safe. For the moment. "I need to get back to TorJake."

"Why? Won't they be all over the ranch?" Her violet eyes were enormous. "Isn't that the last place we should go?"

"They'll be watching at the very least. And we're out of options."

He glanced around, keeping an eye on a homeless man curled up near the underbrush. "Out here, there are too many factors outside of my control."

"What if they're already there waiting? With

everything that's happened so far, they will be all over the place. If the police don't catch us first."

"It's a big ranch. I know a place we can hide for a while as long as we can get supplies."

"You think they have the police in their pockets?"

Caleb scratched behind Max's ears. "There could be an officer on Kane's payroll, not the entire force. Rich, connected people use any means to get what they want. Doesn't matter. He has his own personal army of security to command. I can't watch our backs out here."

"What if the sheriff is there? What if he's waiting to arrest us?"

"He believes you're being set up, too."

Shock widened her eyes. "He said that?"

"Yes."

"How can we be sure he's telling the truth? I mean, he could set a trap to make us feel safe so he can arrest us. Or Kane might have gotten to him, offering cash."

Caleb paused for a beat. "I believe the sheriff is honest. I've known him long enough to vouch for him." Caleb and Coleman might have had a good relationship in the past. But that was before Caleb was wanted for questioning in a murder. It'd be risky to trust Coleman now that they were on the run and wanted for questioning, but he didn't want to tell her that. They couldn't risk being delayed at the station and losing time in their search for Noah. Her fingers were interlocked. "If this guy is as big as you say he is, who can really protect us? Where can we go? Even if we make it to the ranch by some miracle, how will we survive? We'll be in hiding forever."

"Only until we come up with a better plan. I can connect with Matt and the boys. They'll be able to help."

"And Noah will end up dead. I heard him wheeze on the phone. If these men are as heartless as you say, then they won't take him to the hospital. They'll just let him die and dump him somewhere."

"We'll figure out a way to get medicine to the drop. Then we have to hide. I didn't see anything on the CD that will help us."

She folded her arms across her chest. Her hands gripped her elbows until her knuckles went white. "They can't contact me now, remember? Not after you trashed my cell. If I don't show up to the drop and stay, they will kill him. There's no other way to reach me."

"We don't know that. If you go, they'll shoot you on the spot. Then what?"

She looked as though she needed a moment to digest his words. "Why do you think they went from trying to make contact with us to trying to kill us?"

"My guess is whatever Leann had over them, they think you've seen it."

"Will they hurt Noah now anyway?"

"I believe they'll keep him alive until…"

"They finish the job. Meaning, erase both of us. Then they'll kill him."

Caleb looked into her vivid gaze. The hurt he saw nearly did him in. He leaned toward her and rested his forehead against hers.

Her hand came up to his chin and guided his lips to hers.

Those lips, soft and slick, pushed all rational thought aside. The bulge in his jeans tightened and strained. The thought of how good she would feel naked and underneath him crashed into his thoughts like a rogue wave, making him harder. He wanted to lay her down and give her all the comfort she could handle.

Was this a bad idea? How could it be when it felt this right? She was almost too much for him. Too beautiful. Too impossible to resist. Were her emotions strapped on a roller coaster she didn't sign up to ride? Was she afraid? Acting on primal instinct?

She needed confirmation of life. Could he hope for more? That she wanted him as badly as he wanted to feel her naked skin against his?

Her tongue dipped in his mouth, and his control

obliterated. Blood rushed in his ears, overshadowing rational thought.

His body was tuned to hers. Every vibration. Every quick breath. Every sexy little moan. The thin cotton material of her shirt was the only barrier to bare skin. He slipped his hand up her shirt, sliding under her lacy bra where he found her delicate skin. Her nipple pebbled. A whoosh sounded in his ears. His muscles clenched.

He wanted her. *Now.* He pushed deeper into the vee of her legs. Her legs wrapped around his waist. He was so close to her sweetness, he nearly blew it right there.

She flattened her hands against his back, pulling him closer.

His chest flush with hers sent heat and impulse rocketing through him.

Much more and he couldn't stop himself from ripping her clothes off right then and there.

She needed him to think clearly. Not like some teenager drunk on pheromones. Besides, she already wore the weight of the world on her shoulders. He didn't need to add to her guilt.

With a shudder, he pulled back. "I'm sorry."

"Me, too."

"I don't think this is a good idea."

"Oh." Embarrassment flushed her cheeks.

He hadn't meant for that to happen. "Believe me, I *want* this."

"No. You're right. I should definitely not have done that." Her solemn tone of voice sent a ripple through him.

He stood to face her. "I didn't mean to hurt you. All I want to do is help."

She stalked to a tree, putting distance between them. Her beautiful face, the pout of her lips, stirred another inappropriate sexual reaction. Didn't she realize his restraint took Herculean effort at this point?

Dammit that he wanted nothing more than to lay her down right then and make love to her until she screamed his name aloud over and over again. It was all he could do not to think about the pink cotton panties she wore. He hadn't dared buy her another pale blue silky pair.

Hell, the need to hold her and to protect her surged so strongly, he'd almost blown it. He was trying to be a better person and show self-discipline. Last thing he wanted was to take advantage of her vulnerability and have her regretting anything about the time they spent together.

When they made love—correction, *if* they made love—it would be the best damn thing either of them had ever done. She wouldn't walk out of his life afterward. It wouldn't be temporary. *Where the hell did that come from?* The admission shocked him.

What was he thinking exactly?

That he didn't want a convenient relationship with her. Wouldn't she leave when the heat was off and she could return to her normal life? She was used to living in a busy major metropolitan city. Life on TorJake was simple. Hard work. Long days. Lots of paperwork.

Caleb didn't get out much. He didn't hit the bars or see the need to sit at white-tablecloth restaurants.

He loved a hard day's work. A cool shower. A down-home meal. And to wrap his arms around the woman he loved. Life didn't get any better than that.

Simply put, their worlds were too different and when she got her life back—and she would get her life back—wouldn't she walk out like the others and move on? Just like Cissy had? One look at Katherine made his heart stir. Not to mention other parts of his body.

He grunted.

This time, his heart might not recover. He felt more for Katherine in the few days he'd known her than he'd ever felt for his ex-girlfriend.

And that scared the hell out of him.

KATHERINE RUBBED TO ease the chill bumps on her arms. Her attraction to Caleb was a distraction. His square jaw. Those rich brown-gold eyes reminded her why fall was her favorite season. He was so damn sexy. With his body flush to hers, everything tingled and surged.

The wind had picked up and the threat of rain intensified. There was a breeze blowing now with pockets of cooler air blasting her. The temperature between her and Caleb had shifted, too. The question was why?

Not that any of this mattered. Those men would find them. They were going to kill her, Caleb and Noah.

She glanced at her watch. "If we're going to make the drop, we'd better get going."

He shook his head. "Not a good idea."

"I don't have a choice. Noah won't survive without his medicine. I have to get it to him."

"You can't save him if you're dead. You have to know it's a setup. I won't allow them to hurt you."

She bristled. "I have to go."

"I don't like it. They've set a trap."

"At least I'll be in the middle of a busy mall."

"That won't stop them. It's absolutely out of the question. They won't allow anything to happen to Noah as long as you're alive. They know it's the only leverage they have. They let him die and there's no deal."

Katherine had to figure out a way to drop the medicine, especially since she didn't have the file. Didn't he understand she had to take the risk? Those jerks may very well be setting her up. What could she do about it? Bottom line? If she didn't show, what chance did Noah have?

She couldn't allow that to happen. She would have to convince Caleb.

"I need to find a phone so I can make contact with Matt. He'll give me a pulse on the sheriff."

"You can use Leann's."

"Lost the power cord. Besides, they don't know we have it yet. Best leave it that way."

Katherine stood and wobbled. "My ankle hurts. I don't think I can walk anymore." She sat on the nearest rock.

Caleb took a knee in front of her. "Let me see what we have here."

"No. You go on." She glanced around and propped her leg on a big rock. "I need a few minutes."

Trepidation and concern played out over his features. "I guess you'll be okay while I scout the area. I'll leave supplies in case you need anything while I'm gone."

Good. She needed to think. "I'll be fine until you get back. Besides, we have a long journey ahead of us later when we head back to the ranch."

He issued a sharp sigh. "Fine." He looked down at Max. "C'mon, boy."

The little dog scampered to Caleb's feet.

"I'll take him so he doesn't make any noise or draw attention to you. We'll be right back. In the meantime, I want you to stay put. No one can track you here. Stay low and hidden." He motioned toward the thicket. "You'll be safe until I get back."

Safe was a word Katherine figured could be deleted from her vocabulary. Without Caleb, she feared she would never be safe again.

As soon as Caleb was out of sight, she organized supplies.

The sound of Noah wheezing on the phone earlier hammered through her. Time was running out for both of them.

Chapter Nine

Caleb tugged the ball cap he'd bought low on his forehead and put on sunglasses, hooding his eyes. An ache had started in his chest the moment he left Katherine. The memory of her kiss burned into his lips.

It was too early to have real feelings for her. Wasn't it? Protectiveness was a given with her circumstances. His desire to help would be strong. She was in serious trouble. But real feelings?

Not this soon.

Katherine was at the right place at the right time. His wounds from Cissy were still too exposed. She'd got him thinking about what it would be like to have little feet running around the Tor-Jake.

Except that he never missed Cissy the way he was missing Katherine.

Even so, Cissy must've primed him for thinking about having his own family someday and a woman like Katherine by his side. He couldn't deny how right her hands had felt on his body back there.

Hell's bells.

Katherine wasn't interested in a relationship with him. She'd been clear on that.

Maybe this was his twisted way of missing his ex-girlfriend.

Caleb redirected his thoughts as he broke through the tree line and located a phone two blocks away in heavy traffic.

He looked up in time to see a young blonde in tattered jeans and a blouse heading straight toward him. Her backpack had been tossed over her shoulder and her keys were clipped to the strap. A college student? He was most likely in the West Village near the main Southern Methodist University campus. He thought for a second about how close they were to the drop spot and glanced around to see if anyone looked suspicious. Kane could have men stationed anywhere. And they could look like anyone. Even the pretty young woman standing in front of him, stroking the dog, could be a threat. Caleb eyed her.

"Awww. What a cute puppy," she said.

Last thing he wanted was to attract attention. He kept his head low and nodded.

"What's his name?"

"Max." Caleb tensed. His gaze fixed on her,

looking for any hint of a weapon. If she had a gun tucked somewhere, he'd see it.

Then again, Kane hadn't exactly been subtle so far.

"He's a sweetie." She bent down and nuzzled Max's nose. "Aren't you?"

Caleb scanned the area, watching for anything that stood out. The street was busy. The sidewalk cafés were full. This section of Dallas teemed with life. It would be so easy to blend in here.

Her gaze came up, stopping on Caleb's face. "You look familiar. Do I know you?"

"Don't think so." He smiled and paused for a beat. "I better get him back to his mom." An image of Katherine waiting in his bed popped into his thoughts. *Not the time. Or the place.*

The girl smiled and walked away.

Caleb picked up the phone and called Matt.

His buddy answered on the first ring.

"I don't have much time to talk, so I'll make this quick—"

"Caleb? What the hell's going on? Where are you?" Matt was silent for a beat. "Never mind. Don't answer that. We probably have company on the line."

Caleb hadn't thought about the line being tapped. It made sense someone would be listening in and trying to locate him by any means possible. Katherine's little sister had done far worse than take a bat to a hornets' nest. She'd written death warrants for everyone she loved and anyone else who tried to help them. Finding a hiding spot was next to impossible when Kane seemed to have so many people in his pockets. "What's happening at the ranch?"

"The men in suits have been here twice. Whatever she stirred up has gone downright crazy."

"Did you catch the news?"

"Sure did. I know you didn't have anything to do with what they're saying. You couldn't have. I don't care what the witness says," Matt said solemnly.

"Thanks for the confidence. It all happened right in front of me."

"You were there?"

"Unfortunately, yes. One minute I was talking to her. The next, bullets were flying. Surely the investigators will be able to figure out which direction the bullets were fired."

"We'll do whatever we have to, to clear your name." Matt issued a sigh. "There's something I should tell you."

"What's that?"

"A man came by the other day. Said he was a U.S. Marshal. He's offering witness protection to her," Matt whispered. "Said he'd already offered it to her sister."

"What else did he say?"

"He can work out a deal for you, too. Put you both in the program."

"You know I won't leave my ranch," Caleb said, steadfast.

"Well, you might have to. This thing has blown up beyond big."

"Did Coleman meet with him?"

"Yes."

He knew the sheriff was honest to a fault. If he trusted the stranger, then Caleb could risk a little faith, too. Not even a man with Kane's pull could persuade Coleman to switch teams. "What did he think?"

"Said the guy checked out. Thinks you should talk to him. And, Caleb, I do, too."

Then again, the guy working for a legitimate agency didn't mean he was clean. Maybe Caleb could get a better feel if he spoke to Coleman directly. "Tell the sheriff I'll be in touch."

"Not a good idea. He has a tail. Besides, you're wanted. He said to warn you if he sees you he'll have to detain you."

Caleb should've seen that coming. "I don't have much time. How's the ranch?"

"To hell with that, how are you?"

"I'm good. Don't worry about me. Just take care of my horses until I return."

"You know I will."

"Make sure you check out the property, too.

The teenagers have been hitting the north fence hard. The acreage in the east needs to be checked for coyotes."

"Jimmy's been on it."

"Won't he be off for his daughter's surgery soon?"

"Yeah."

Caleb needed to drop a hint. Tell Matt where he was going. But how? "You better take over for him. And make sure someone's exercising Dawn. Can't have her too restless like before, when Cissy left. No one's been watching that trail she rode and I might not be back for a long time."

"Don't talk like that." He listened carefully for the telltale rise of Matt's voice when he caught on. "We'll get this figured out, and you'll be home before you know it."

Nope. Matt hadn't picked up on the clue. "I wouldn't count on it."

"It will all work out."

Maybe he could send Matt on a mission? "Do me a favor?"

"Name it."

"Find a picture of Sebastian Kane."

"The businessman?"

"Yes. Call the manager of the Coffee Hut in Austin and send him the picture. Find out if he came into the shop much, or spent any time with one of the employees by the name of Leann Foster."

"Consider it done."

"I'll be in touch."

"Be safe, man."

Caleb ended the call. He prayed he'd disconnected before his location had been tagged. Being away from Katherine gave him an uneasy feeling, like dark clouds closing in around him, threatening to take away all that was light and good. He needed to get back and make sure she was all right. With her damaged ankle, she might not be able to run. He'd never forgive himself if anything had happened while he'd been gone.

Keeping his head low, he circled back to the brush where he'd tucked her away.

What the hell?

"Katherine," he called into the nearby shrubbery. He searched branches and bushes. Nothing. No answer.

Fear and anger formed liquid that ran cold in his veins. Had he been careless? Had he left her vulnerable and alone with no way to defend herself? Had the cops picked her up?

The bag of supplies was left leaning against the rock. He checked it. The pain relievers were missing as were several bottled waters.

He called her name again, louder.

"Caleb." Her voice came from his left.

He rushed to the bushes at the edge of the hill. His heart thumped in his throat. "What happened?"

"I slipped on a rock." She was on all fours, climbing up.

He picked her up and carried her to the rock. Relief filled his chest. He didn't want to acknowledge how stressed he'd been a minute ago. "What were you doing over there?"

"Looking for you. My leg gave out and I slipped over the edge."

Glancing at his watch, he swore under his breath. "The drop."

"I'm fine. I can make it."

"You wait here. I'll figure something out."

"No. Please. I can do this." She tugged at his hand. Her eyes pleaded.

Looking into her determined eyes, he knew he couldn't leave her behind. She'd be safer if he kept her within arm's reach until he could get her back to TorJake. "Okay."

Caleb retraced his route to West Village, going as slowly as she needed to.

If memory served, NorthPark Center wasn't far. In fact, it should be on the other side of Highway 75. Easy walk for him. Nothing was easy for Katherine right then.

If they thought she'd showed up alone, and weren't expecting him, the element of surprise would be on his side. The thought of anyone touching her or hurting her sent white-hot anger coursing through him.

Why was she so stubborn?

Didn't she realize she might be walking right into their arms? Being in the open was good. Crowds hid a lot of things.

He didn't know if this was the best play. They were walking into a situation set up by Kane. They didn't have the file. Should he turn and walk away while they still could? Meet with the marshal who'd seemed legit? Because nothing about his current situation was going to turn out the way he wanted. She was far too willing to put herself in harm's way to protect everyone around her. Except this burning desire to help Katherine, to keep her safe, kept his feet moving anyway.

People didn't accidently get mixed up with a man like Kane. What was the connection?

Caleb chewed on that thought as he led Katherine a few blocks, near the meeting site.

"Let me go first. Get a good read." Caleb ran ahead and entered the grassy area, leaving her at the perimeter. He blended in with the noisy lunch crowd.

Scanning the area, he could see at least five shooters in position.

Kane had come prepared to do anything necessary to erase Katherine.

If she took a couple more steps, she'd be right where they wanted her.

An imposing figure made a move toward her.

Caleb crouched low. When she stepped into his sight, he sprang forward and clutched her hand. She was shaking.

He pulled her into the crowd.

Glancing around, the shooters didn't seem to notice the small commotion. He turned to a teen and tapped his shoulder. "Hey, kid."

The teen glanced up, looking annoyed at the interruption. When he saw Caleb, the teen straightened his back and pulled out his earbuds.

"Sorry to bother you while you're listening to your music, buddy. I was wondering if you'd like to make a quick twenty bucks."

The kid eyed Caleb suspiciously.

"I need to deliver this stuff to the bronze statue." Caleb took the medicines from Katherine's tight grip. She stroked Max.

The boy's face twisted, giving the universal teenage sign for, *Have you lost your mind?* "Mister, that's only, like, twenty feet away."

Caleb smiled and winked. "It's a dollar a step basically. You want the job or not?"

"Sure. I'd kiss your mother for twenty bucks."

"Deliver the medicine. And leave my mother out of it."

The teen palmed the pill bottle and inhaler. "That's it?"

Caleb nodded.

"Deal."

"Be inconspicuous and I'll make it forty."

A wide smile broke across the teen's face. "Then I'll be stealth."

He rocked his head back and forth as he walked to the sculpture. His gaze intent on the music device in his hand, he plopped down next to the statue.

Caleb never saw the kid slip the medicine under the bronze, but as soon as he popped to his feet and strolled away the package stood out. Amazing.

"Nice job, kid." Caleb handed him a pair of twenties. He had no idea what Kane and his men would do when they realized there was no file.

"Pleasure doing business with you," he said as he turned and then sauntered off.

With his hand on Katherine's shoulder, he guided her toward a tour group. "Let's get out of here before anyone gets hurt."

"I—I can't. Not without knowing if they got his med—"

"See that baby over there?" He pointed to a mother nursing an infant. "They both could die if we don't leave now."

A mix of emotions played across her features. Worry. Guilt. Her stubborn streak was visible on the surface as her chin lifted. "You're right."

No sooner had the words left her mouth than a cufflelike noise moved toward them. People ran different directions, parting faster than the Red

Sea, as a serious-looking man walked down the middle. Sunglasses hooded his eyes, but his intention was clear. His face didn't veer from Katherine.

Caleb grabbed her by the arm and pushed her ahead of him, placing himself in between her and the suit. If he could get her toward the flagship store, maybe they could get lost in the rows of clothing.

As they neared the wide-open door, two similar-looking men in suits flanked the entrance.

They were trapped. The man from behind was closing in on them fast. Glancing from left to right, Caleb looked for another way out. One side was a brick wall. Nothing there.

A police radio broke the silence from the left-hand side. Not good.

Except.

Wait a minute.

That would work.

Caleb ducked toward the officer and waved his hands wildly. "I'd like to turn myself in."

"What are you doing?" Katherine's expression was mortification personified.

"Trust me," was all he said.

The look she gave him said she thought he'd snapped. Lost his mind. Her concern that this would make Kane kill Noah was written in the worry lines on her face. The thought crossed Caleb's mind, too. He had to take the chance or they would all be dead. Besides, Kane would most likely bide his time. If he killed Noah too soon, he would lose all his leverage.

Caleb squeezed her hand. "I know what I'm doing."

Too late. The officer was next to them in a beat. "Katherine Harper?"

"Yes, sir," Caleb said.

Katherine's bewildered expression must've robbed her of her ability to speak, too.

"I believe we're wanted for questioning." Caleb glanced around.

The men had disappeared.

Caleb didn't realize until that moment that he'd been holding his breath.

KATHERINE ALLOWED CALEB to lead her outside the police station. Being detained for the past twenty-four hours heightened her fatigue. "You didn't say anything about Noah, did you?"

"No. I didn't figure you wanted me to. Thought about it, though."

"So did I. I actually expected to be arrested."

"That might come next. They're still gathering and analyzing evidence. What did you tell them?"

"That we didn't do anything wrong. I explained exactly how it all happened back at my apartment. Said it must be some mistake. A random act of violence."

"So did I. The crime scene evidence should corroborate our story."

"There's no way they'll let Noah go if I involve the police. Kane will be furious at me for evading him at the drop for sure now. He warned me to come alone."

"Yes. But Noah will be alive and so will you." Caleb's forehead was etched with worry. Lines bracketed his mouth as he set Max down in a patch of grass.

"You're right. I probably haven't seemed very appreciative. I hope you know how very grateful I am. None of this would have happened without you. Noah and I would probably both be dead by now."

He squeezed her hand reassuringly. He didn't speak. His focus shifted from face to face as though he was evaluating threats.

Katherine exhaled deeply.

He wrapped his arms around her. She was flush with his chest before she could blink.

He pressed a kiss to her forehead. "It was stupid of us to walk into Kane's trap. I thought, for a second, I might lose you. Turning ourselves in was a risk I had to take to get us out of there and keep us alive."

Panic came off his frame in palpable waves.

Fear dilated his pupils. His dark brown eyes sliced through her pain. Her loneliness. Katherine didn't realize how alone she'd been until Caleb. "I'm here. I'm not going away. Not unless you want me to."

"No. I don't. I want you right here with me."

She felt comforted by his strong presence. One hand slipped up his shirt onto his chest, rubbing against his skin in the hope of calming him.

She pressed her face against his cotton T-shirt before placing a kiss on his chest. "I'm right here."

He smiled. His fingers tangled in her hair, stroking it off her face.

He splayed his hand on her bottom, lighting fires from deep inside her. He lowered his face to hers and kissed her. His lips skimmed across hers and lit nerve endings she didn't know existed. Her body zinged to life, tantalized, pulsing volts of heat. A little piece of her heart wished he'd said forever.

A car alarm sounded.

He took a step back and scanned the parking lot, picking up Max. "I spoke to Matt."

Katherine tried to regain her mental balance because for a moment she got lost…lost in his gaze… lost in all that was Caleb. "What did he say?"

"Apparently your sister was talking to the Feds. There's a guy who seems legit. He's offering witness protection to you."

"What about you?"

Caleb shrugged. "Don't need it."

"You would never leave TorJake, would you?"

"It's the only home I've ever known."

Katherine hadn't felt home in so many years she couldn't count. Except that lately, home felt a lot like wherever Caleb was. But that was ridiculous. They'd only just met. It took years of getting to know someone before a bond like that could be created. Running for her life, trying to beat bullets, defying death probably had toyed with her emotions. No doubt, she had feelings for Caleb. That couldn't be denied. But the kinds of feelings that could last a lifetime? Real love? Wouldn't he let her down like the others had?

"Can't say I know what you mean," she lied. "How do we know this man can be trusted?"

Caleb's expression was weary. "I thought about that, too. I don't know. It might be the best chance we have."

"What about Noah? What will they do for him?"

"Good question. This guy said he was trying to help your sister before her accident. If they safely tuck you away, he can go after Noah."

"What do you think I should do?" Katherine turned the tables.

His pupils dilated for a split second as the muscles in his jaw clenched. It was the look he got when he was holding back what he really wanted to say.

"Whatever it takes to stay alive," he said, deadpan.

"So you think I should just turn myself in. Let the government handle this?" How could he say this to her? Hadn't he just told her to stay with him? Why had his gaze suddenly cooled?

"I didn't say that. You have to make the decision for yourself. I tried to drop a hint to Matt of where we'd be. We won't survive long without supplies and neither one of us knows how many of Kane's men are out there. Matt didn't get it."

"Where can we go? The police aren't looking for us right now. But Kane's men won't let up."

"I still think the ranch is the best place. There's a spot no one checks on the far side of the property."

"Then I want to go with you."

"Does that mean you won't turn yourself over to federal protection?"

She crossed her arms over her chest. "No. And it's not up for discussion right now."

"I told Matt to talk to Leann's boss to see if Kane visited the coffee shop."

"Good idea." As she turned to walk away, she could feel Caleb's presence right behind her. She was tempted to lean back against his chest and allow him to wrap his arms around her. She didn't.

Whatever Leann had gotten involved with had to have been by accident. No way had her sister known this Kane person. She didn't get involved with known criminals or men with this kind of influence. Leann could keep a secret but she wouldn't drag herself and Noah into a mess like this. "She must've seen something horrible to cause all this."

"I was thinking the same thing. She was a witness to a crime. It's the only reason she'd be offered federal protection that I know of," he said quietly. "We need to make contact with the marshal to figure out what exactly."

Relief and vindication washed over Katherine. The emotions were followed by a deep sense of sadness.

Caleb stroked Max's fur. "I recognized one of the men earlier from photographs in the newspaper at the police station. He was definitely one of Kane's entourage."

"They'll keep coming until they find us, won't they?"

"I believe so."

Tears stung her eyes. What kind of horrible man had her nephew? And yet, Noah had sounded okay on the phone. "Think they picked up his med' cine?"

"He's of no value dead. They kill him and yo

go into witness protection. They might have found out Leann was considering the program."

"Do you think they killed her? And they had to get to her before she disappeared with the evidence?" A chill raced up Katherine's arms. "Why not kill me and Noah, too?"

He shrugged. "They think you have evidence. Two sisters and a little boy dead in a short time would sound alarms."

"I just can't figure out why she didn't go right in. Why would she wait?" A beat passed. "For Noah, I guess. She didn't want him to have that life. Kane must not have known about him before."

"Or she didn't think he did."

Reality dawned on her. "Leann was planning to leave him with me before she disappeared. She wanted to make sure he was safe. I'll bet she was ready to turn herself in."

"She must've figured they wouldn't connect the two of you. But why?"

"Leann changed her name when she left all those years ago, so we had different last names. It was her way of cutting all ties." She paused. "Still want to go to your ranch?"

"Yes."

"Then let's go."

"First, we need to change your appearance," he said solemnly, tugging on his hat.

"Good idea. I almost didn't recognize you when you showed up. Max gave you away." She scratched him behind the ears, grateful the police hadn't taken him from her as she recognized the area as their original hiding spot.

"The ball cap. Small changes can make a big difference." He pulled a scarf from the bag of supplies.

She covered most of her hair and tied a knot in the back to hold the material in place. "How's this?"

He tucked a stray strand inside the fabric. "I wouldn't say better. You'd be beautiful no matter what you wore. This is different. Different is good. We want different."

His touch connected her to the memory of his hands on her before. His urgency. Ecstasy. She had no doubt those big hands could bring her pleasures she'd never known.

She ignored the sensitized shivers skittering across her nerves. "A man like Kane won't give up easily, will he?" She lowered her gaze.

He lifted her chin until she was looking him in the eye again. "Don't be sorry for any of this. I'm not. You didn't ask for this any more than Noah did. I'm sure your parents would be proud of you right now. You're risking your life to save your sister's boy. There's no shame in that."

"Except I feel like a coward."

His rich brown gaze trained on her. "Then you don't see what I do."

"Then what am I?"

"Strong. Brave. Intelligent."

She felt a blush crawl up her neck to her cheeks. "You make me sound like so much more than I feel right now."

"Sometimes the brain plays tricks on us. We don't have to buy into it. That's our choice."

She looked him dead in the eye. "You think we'll be safe at your ranch?"

He nodded. "For a while anyway."

Katherine was certain they'd be caught.

If not by Kane's men, then eventually by the Feds. The government wouldn't give a free pass to fugitives. Murderers. If Kane had his way, that would be the label put on them by everyone. Police. Reporters. Citizens. Anyone and everyone.

Strangers would be afraid of them.

Her life was shattered. There'd be no going back.

A new identity didn't sound like a bad idea. She doubted she'd have a job left to go back to when all this was said and done anyway. Would her friends and boss believe she'd had nothing to do with the murder of her landlady?

Friends? That was a joke. Katherine kept to herself most of the time. She worked and read and kept people at a distance, didn't she?

Except for her cowboy.

How could he push her toward the program? Didn't that mean they'd never see each other again?

Her lip quivered, but she ignored it. "I'm tired of running scared. They always seem a step ahead of me anyway."

A mischievous twinkle intensified his gold-brown eyes. "Are you saying what I think you are?"

"I'm ready to fight back."

Caleb's face brightened with anticipation. His eyes glittered an incredible shade of brown. "It's risky."

Risky didn't cover the half of it to Katherine. And yet, waiting, not knowing what would happen next, giving the other guys all the advantage wasn't an option, either. She'd been letting Kane and his men hold the cards for too long. Time to take control. "I know."

"You're sure about this?"

"I've never been more certain of anything in my life. I'm not sure what the plan is yet. Just that we need one."

"Then let's give 'em hell."

He got a sexy spark in his eye when he was

being bad. How could someone become so special to her in such a short time span?

She couldn't imagine doing any of this without Caleb. Her cowboy protector…friend…*lover?*

Chapter Ten

Caleb needed transportation. Walking around outside exposed wasn't good, especially after Katherine's fall. Her ankle was swelling again. Kane's men would be all over the place now that they'd managed to get away from them. He was half surprised no one had waited outside the police station earlier. Could he get Katherine out of the city safely before Kane figured out they'd been released?

Even though they'd been questioned and released, being identified by a random person could put them both in danger. Especially if one of Kane's men was around. Attracting attention wasn't good.

He located the nicest restaurant in the area; intently watched where the valet parked cars. He scanned the parking garage for witnesses. A family stepped out of the elevator. He froze. A stab of guilt hit him. He didn't like the idea of taking someone else's property, but there was no other choice. Steal or die.

When the valet parked an SUV with the windows blacked out, he waited for the family to unload their minivan and the valet to jog out of sight.

Caleb figured the owner would be in the restaurant for a good hour. That should give them enough time to get out of the city before anyone knew the sport utility was missing. He could ditch the SUV in a field or alley outside of Allen. If he could get that far, he'd be close enough to get home on foot. The less walking the better for Katherine. Even with a modest amount of pain reliever, she had to be hurting.

He put on a pair of sterile gloves and felt the back tire on the driver's side. Jackpot. The keys were there. A trick he'd learned back in the day before he'd gone on the straight and narrow.

The ignition caught and he drove the SUV to pick up Katherine and Max a minute later.

"I don't want to know where you got this, do I?" She slid into the passenger seat next to him.

"Probably not."

"Then I won't ask." She smiled. Her violet eyes darkened, reflecting her exhaustion. She was putting up a brave front. He could see the fear lurking behind her facade.

He merged the SUV into traffic a few moments

later, disappearing onto Highway 75. "Why don't you put the seat back and rest?"

She eyed him warily. "How did you find this so easily?"

There was no use lying to her. "I have a record. Got into trouble as a kid. Had reasons to know how to lift a car quickly." He looked at her more intently, needing to know if his admission bothered her. "I did all that stuff a long time ago. I would never do it now. Hank helped me straighten up."

She didn't blink. "Seems like he also taught you some useful skills for staying alive."

"Any decent man would help a woman in this situation."

"Am I just any woman?"

Was she?

He wanted to continue to compare her to Cissy, the others, needing something to tamp down the out-of-control reaction his body was having. "I never said that."

"Never mind. You've been my knight in shining armor. Which falls into the 'any decent man' category." Her smile didn't reach her eyes.

He wanted to be more to her than "any decent man." But he couldn't ignore the realities. Katherine was a woman in trouble. Cissy had been in dire straits when she'd showed up at his door, too. She'd cried and begged him to help. He would've done anything to save that little girl of hers. Cissy hadn't needed to grovel. And yet, she'd begged to stay at the ranch. Said Savannah loved it out there. When he'd arranged all the doctor visits and taken over her medical care, Cissy had become even more attached.

She'd played a good hand. Turned on the tears when he hadn't immediately returned the sentiment.

Caleb had been convinced her feelings were real. Even though he'd believed getting involved would be a bad idea, she'd eventually worn him down. One thing was certain, he'd do it all again if it meant saving Savannah.

Did he have a deep-down need to save women?

He figured a shrink would have a field day with his psyche. They'd probably say he rescued women because he hadn't been able to save his mom. They'd be right about the last part. Caleb hadn't been able to stop the bastard who'd fathered him from hurting his mother. If Caleb had been older... gotten his bare hands around that man's neck... Caleb would have ripped the guy's head off.

He'd been too young. Too weak. The old man was bigger. Stronger.

Caleb saw too much of the jerk in himself when he looked into the mirror. Let the bastard show his face now. Why did they have to look so much alike?

He couldn't go back and change what made him the man he was today any more than he could stop himself from doing what he thought was right.

Katherine's delicate hand on his arm redirected his attention.

Caleb couldn't ignore the bolt of heat shooting through him from where she touched. She stirred emotions he'd sworn not to feel again. And yet, how could he stop himself?

Cissy hadn't been gone long. She'd left a hole. Was he trying to fill it with Katherine?

"Where'd you go just now?"

"I'm right here."

"You're not getting off that easily, buster. You know all about my situation. Now it's your turn. Talk."

"You don't want to know what I was thinking."

Her violet eyes widened as she sat up. "Why not? Does it have to do with me?"

Katherine was brave and caring. Even when she was afraid, she faced it. She hadn't asked for his help. In fact, she'd been leery of accepting any aid. Every step of the way, she thought of others, not considering herself during this entire ordeal. When they were both hurt, she wanted to attend to his wounds first. The guilt she carried was a heavy weight on her back. She didn't use tears as a weapon. No, she refused to cry. She held everything on her shoulders and rarely let him in.

When he really thought about it, the comparison to Cissy didn't hold water.

Katherine was nothing like Cissy.

He didn't have any plans to tell Katherine how much she occupied his thoughts.

"Maybe I should drive. You haven't slept in a couple of days now. All the adrenaline must be wearing off, too. I'm sure your body's as worn down as mine," she said. "Probably more so since you haven't so much as closed your eyes since this whole ordeal started."

"I'm fine."

"Still, I'd feel much better if you got some rest. You have dark circles under your eyes. Let me take the wheel for a while."

"I appreciate your concern." She had no idea how much he meant those words.

The back of her hand came up to press against the stubble on his face. Desire pounded him, tensing his muscles and demanding release. A dull ache formed at his temples.

No way was he acting on it in the car.

Maybe soon…

"Besides, we have to ditch the sport utility," he said.

She moved to the backseat. He noticed her taut legs and sweet round behind as she climbed over.

"Here, the least I can do is rub your shoulders."

She worked his tense muscles. Having her hands

on him created the opposite effect she desired. Instead of relaxing, his body went rigid. His need for her surged, causing his neck muscles to become more tense.

He glanced in the rearview mirror in time to see her frown.

"You're so tense. That can't be good."

A grin tugged at the corners of his mouth. She had no idea the effect she was having on him. "You touch me much more like that and I can't be held responsible for my actions."

Her eyes widened as reality dawned on her.

Was that a smile he just saw cross her features?

"I DIDN'T MEAN to create an issue for you," Katherine said, quashing the self-satisfied smirk trying to force its way to the surface. She enjoyed the fact a man so strong, so powerful, reacted so intensely to her lightest touch.

"Well you have," he said with a killer grin.

Damn he was sexy.

Katherine forced her gaze away from him and climbed into the front seat.

The sexually charged air hung thickly between them, sending her body to crackling embers. Had she ever felt this way for a man before?

No. Never.

And a tiny piece of her couldn't help but wonder if she'd ever feel this way again. Or if she'd live long enough to see where it could go. Noah. Baby. She prayed he had the life-saving medicine he needed by now.

"This looks like a good place to ditch the SUV," he said, pulling into a corn field.

"Then what?"

"We walk from here. Unless we get lucky and find an ATV."

About the last thing Katherine felt was lucky. "What are the chances of that happening?"

"Pretty good actually. When you know where to look." There came that devilish smile again.

It sent Katherine's heart pounding and her thighs burning to have him nestled against her. She sighed. More inappropriate thoughts. They were becoming more difficult to contain. Caleb was one powerful man. His presence had a way of electrifying her senses and causing her to want. She knew better. Her body wanted nothing more than to get into bed with him and allow his strong physical presence to cover her, warm her and protect her.

Her logical mind knew to rail against those primal feminine urges.

She opened the door, but Caleb was already there. He took Max, and let him run free.

"We'll be okay for a minute. Let me check that ankle before you try to walk on it."

He closed his hand around her ankle and she

ignored the fires he lit there, focusing instead on the little dog.

Max piddled on a nearby cornstalk and scurried back to Caleb's feet.

Smart dog. He seemed to know on instinct who the alpha male was.

She took in a deep breath to clear her mind but only managed to breathe in his scent. He was outdoors and masculinity and sex personified. *Bad idea.*

Katherine gripped her purse. "How terrible is it?"

"Are you in pain?"

"A little." She blocked out the true wound. The cavern that couldn't be filled in her chest if anything happened to Noah...or if she couldn't be with Caleb. Her ankle was nothing in comparison to those hurts. "I'll be able to walk on it."

"It's pretty swollen. I'd hate to make it worse."

"Not much choice." She smiled. "We can't hide out in a cornfield forever."

"I was trying to decide if I should let you walk or carry you."

"Oh, don't do that." The very thought of his hands on her sent a sensual chill up her back. The feeling of his arms wrapped around her would be nice. No doubt about it. But if her body was pressed to his, he'd read every bit of physical reaction she had to him. That couldn't possibly help matters.

Katherine squared her shoulders. "No can do, captain. I'm ready and willing to walk the plank."

Her attempt at humor fell flat. *Can't blame a girl for trying.* Where had that come from? She was becoming delirious. It would do her good to focus. Walking, painful as it would be, would also keep her on track and feeling alive.

Noah's kidnapping came crashing down on Katherine's thoughts.

I won't let you down, baby.

"You mind staying here while I look for transportation?" Caleb asked, breaking through.

"Not at all." She took out a bottle of water and sipped before pouring a little in her curled hand for Max. "Besides, I have company."

Max ignored the water and followed Caleb as he walked away, leaving the water to run off her palm.

Two-timing little puff ball.

Not that she could blame the dog, really. If she had a choice between being protected by her or Caleb, she'd choose the hunky guy with sex appeal to spare, too.

With Caleb by her side, they'd deflected bullets and escaped crazy killers, and yet he'd managed to keep them both alive. If she had money to put on a horse, that Thoroughbred would be named Caleb Snow.

Katherine opened her bag. The pic of Leann with baby Noah she'd taken from the apartment stared up at her. A lump formed in her throat, making it difficult to swallow. She wanted to cry. To feel the sweet release of tears. To liberate all the bottled-up feelings swelling in her chest and let everything go. Nothing came.

Katherine was the emotional equivalent of a drought.

CALEB'S LUCK IMPROVED considerably when he located the ATV at the edge of the field. He roared up with it, enjoying the feeling of making Katherine smile. She looked from Max to Caleb. The little dog had perched its front paws on the steering column and wagged his tail as soon as Katherine came into view.

What could Caleb say? The dog had good taste.

He helped her onto the back and secured her arms around his midsection.

Fifteen minutes into the ride, the ATV stalled. "Out of gas." Going on foot from here would frustrate anyone who was able to follow their tracks.

"Me, too," she said with a brilliant smile. The kind of smile that made a man think she possessed all the stars in the heavens and they reflected like stardust from her face. Wasn't like him to wax poetic.

He made a crutch for her out of a thick tree branch, urging her to put her weight on him as Max tagged along behind, keeping pace.

"Where are we headed?" Katherine asked as they pushed deeper into the woods.

"There's an old building at the back of my property. It's the original homestead. Not much more than a couple of rooms. Been empty for years. No one ever goes there. Hell, few people even know it exists it's so far to the edge of my property. I like it that way, too. I keep a few basic supplies, blankets and such, in the place in case I get out here riding fences and don't want to come back."

"What could you possibly have to hide from? The world? Why? You have a beautiful ranch. Your life looks perfect to me."

Not exactly. There was no one like her waiting for him when he came home every night.

His adrenaline had faded, and he was running out of juice. Especially with the way his mind kept wandering to thoughts of her. What he'd like to do to her.

The rest of the long walk was quiet.

Relief flooded him as the building came into view. A few more steps and he could get Katherine off her bad leg.

He opened the door, and put a thick blanket on

top of the wood platform he'd frequently used as a bed. The place had gotten a fair amount of use when Cissy had left. Plenty of times, Caleb hadn't wanted to be inside the main house. She'd disappeared in such a hurry she hadn't packed. Her things were left in the bedroom. Savannah's toys littered the grounds. Reminders of his life with them had been everywhere. They'd been like land mines to Caleb. Each one had detonated a memory…brought out the hollow feeling in his chest. He hadn't been able to look at the color purple again without seeing Savannah's stuffed hippo. It went with her everywhere, tucked under her arm. When she'd watch TV, the hippo was her pillow.

"At least tell me why you have so many things out here. And I don't believe it's just in case you get restless. I'm sure there are plenty of places you could find to soothe yourself." Her violet eyes tore through him.

"My ex had a little girl. They both left. It broke my heart."

"I'm sorry. She wasn't yours?"

He shook his head, stuffing regret down somewhere deep. "No."

"What happened?"

"When they left, it felt like my heart had been ripped from my chest."

She covered his heart with her hand, connecting to the pain he felt.

"Thought I would suffocate inside the house for how empty it felt. Like the air was in a vacuum and I couldn't breathe."

"You must've loved her."

He nodded. "I'd take my horse, Dawn, out after supper. At times, I couldn't bring myself to go back inside, so I would come here. Guess everyone worried. Matt followed me one night. Margaret probably made him. So, he knows about this place, too."

"Anyone else aware of this place?"

"Me and Matt. Now you."

He settled her onto the blanket and tended to her cuts. He didn't have ice in any of the supplies. There was no electricity at the place. But he'd bought a compression sock at the big-box store and that should help with the swelling. He slipped off her sandal and slid the sock around her foot and up her silky calf. "This should help."

He didn't immediately move his hand. It felt so natural to touch her.

Max circled around a few times before curling up in a ball next to Katherine.

"He lost a lot today. He's probably exhausted," she said.

"So are you." He patted the little puff ball's head.

"I can't help but worry about Noah. I'd close my eyes but I'm afraid of the images my mind will conjure up." The corners of her mouth turned down.

The picture of her when he'd first seen her, all chestnut hair and cherry lips, scared and alone, invaded his thoughts. Her misery was his. He wanted to kiss away her pain. Since he knew he'd never stop there, he went to the small kerosene stove instead and heated water. Margaret had slipped some herbal bags in with his supplies. More of her healing tea no doubt. Caleb was a coffee man, but he was glad for what she'd done. It might provide Katherine with the comfort she needed to relax.

"What's this?" she asked when he handed her a tin cup full of steaming brew.

"Margaret said something about it calming the mind."

"You didn't sleep much after your ex-girlfriend left, did you?" The question caught him off guard.

He shook his head. "I was in bad shape for a while."

He'd rebounded faster than he believed possible thanks to the love and support he received from his second family. Margaret and Matt had been beside him every step of the way until the pain had faded.

He could recall very little about Cissy in detail. He couldn't for the life of him remember what she smelled like, and yet the spring flower bouquet with a hint of vanilla, Katherine's scent, was etched in his memory. Vivid. If she disappeared right then and he never saw her again, he would remember how she smelled for the rest of his life. "I'm better now."

The sound of branches cracking stopped him.

Glancing around, he realized he had nothing to use as a weapon out there. He'd ditched his rifle long ago when he'd run out of ammunition at Katherine's house.

He moved to Katherine and covered her with his body, pulling dusty blankets on top of them to hide.

Even after the outside noise stopped, Caleb held his breath. Matt might have figured out the hint from their earlier phone call, and he could've brought the sheriff with him for all his good intentions. Or it could be an animal.

Katherine lay beneath him, her soft warm body rising and falling with every breath she took, pressing against him. The memory of the way they'd met etched in his thoughts. The way her body felt underneath him. A perfect fit. Her face was so close; he wouldn't have to move far to skim his lips across her jawline, or the base of her throat where he could see her pulse throb. It wouldn't take much movement to lift his chin and kiss her. But he realized he wanted so much more than her kiss.

More than her body.

He wanted all of her. Mind. Body. Soul—if there was such a thing.

Before any of that could happen, he wanted to be able to trust her.

He needed to know that if he opened his heart, she wouldn't stamp her heels all over it and walk away.

The tricky part? To find out, he had to go out on a limb and give the very thing he avoided... trust. Both his father and Cissy had done a number on him in that department. Since history was the best predictor of the future, believing in someone again felt about as easy as skinning a live rattlesnake with a hairbrush.

He wished like hell he'd told Katherine how he'd felt about her when he'd had the chance.

If he could get beyond the pain of his past, could he have a real future with her?

Or would she leave just like the others?

Chapter Eleven

The door to the homestead creaked open slowly. "Caleb, you in here?"

Caleb recognized Matt's voice immediately. He threw the covers off and stood. "Come inside and shut the door."

Worry lines bracketed his friend's mouth. "Damn, I've been worried."

Relief eased Caleb's tense muscles. "I didn't think you'd caught on to my hint on the phone."

"It took me a while. Then it finally clicked."

Caleb helped Katherine into a comfortable sitting position, elevating her swollen ankle. He turned to Matt. "What's going on?"

"You tell me. People are coming out of the woodwork looking for you. Margaret's beside herself with worry."

"No doubt they've been expecting me to come home."

Matt nodded.

"What kind of people have been showing up?"

"The marshal for one. He's been checking in every few hours. I didn't tell him you'd made contact, but he seems to know."

"The line must be tapped."

"I guessed as much."

"Speaking of which, you didn't bring your phone with you, did you?"

Matt shook his head. "Figured if they could get to one, they could get to another. Left it in the barn just in case. Sneaked out the back."

"Good thinking. Kane's men followed our movements with the ones we had. I had to ditch them."

"No wonder I kept rolling into voice mail every time I called."

"Who else has been by the ranch?"

"The men in suits have stopped by several times." His lips formed a grim line. "They're staying in town at the Dovetail Inn."

"Did you tell the marshal about them?"

Matt nodded. "He said to ignore them. Truth is I don't know what or who to believe anymore." His gaze traveled from Caleb to Katherine.

"I do," Caleb said firmly. He sensed this whole ordeal would be coming to a head soon, and a big piece of him dreaded the day he would part company with Katherine. It was selfish. He should want everything to be behind them and for normal life to return. Except that she'd imprinted him in ways he could never have imagined a woman could. Being forced to live without her sounded worse than a death sentence. His heart said she wouldn't walk out, but logic forced him to look at his history.

Then again, if the men with guns had their way, he might not live long enough to miss her. And he would. From somewhere deep inside where a little bit of light still lived within him.

"Either way, I can connect with the marshal if you want to go into the program we talked about." Matt shot another weary glance toward Katherine.

Her chin came up proudly, but to her credit she didn't say anything.

She was strong and bold. Another reason Caleb's argument she was just like Cissy didn't hold up. Damn she was sexy, beautiful and strong. Made him want to kick Matt out and do things to her that would remind her she was all woman and not some errant fugitive destined to die by the hands of some criminal jerk.

"They'll have to take me out of here in a box. I have no plans to leave my ranch again." Closure was coming, one way or another, and Caleb regretted the second he realized it also meant their time together would come to an end. He silently pledged to show her just how appealing she was before that happened. "I won't run anymore."

"Is that such a good idea?" Matt's chin jutted out, and he blew out a breath.

Caleb shrugged. "This is my home."

"I can go. I'll draw them away from you," Katherine said, seeming resigned to her fate.

He was touched but not surprised she'd be willing to put herself in more danger for him. Her current situation had come about because she would give her life to protect her nephew. Yet another difference between her and Cissy. Cissy had only thought about herself.

"I don't mean any disrespect, but she brings up a good point. Maybe if she leaves…"

"It won't matter. I'm still a person of interest in a murder, remember?"

"How could I forget?" Matt said with a disgusted grunt. His gaze intensified on Katherine.

"Enough," Caleb barked to his friend. Frustration was getting the best of him. "Did you have a chance to follow up on the mission we discussed?"

"I did." His face muscles pulled taut. "I called the manager, and asked if I could email him a picture of someone I was looking for. I sent him a photo of Kane from a news article I found. He recognized him right away. Said he came in the coffee shop all the time. Or used to when Leann worked there before the accident."

"I wonder why a man like him would get involved with my sister."

"I already know. The manager put one of her co-workers on the line. She was chatty. Said she and Leann used to go climbing together sometimes. She was with her the day of her accident at Enchanted Rock. They all stood by helplessly when she lost her grip and tumbled...."

Matt fixed his gaze on the floor a second before continuing. "The woman said Leann practically dropped out of sight when her old boyfriend showed up a few months ago."

Katherine gasped. "They dated?"

Caleb closed his hand around hers, looping their fingers together, and offering reassurance so she could hear more. She rewarded him with a weak smile.

"Said they were like two lovebirds. He'd visit her at the coffee shop and drop off presents, flowers." Matt looked from Katherine to Caleb and back. "She also said he's Noah's dad."

Katherine's fingers went limp.

"No," came out on a whisper. "Can't be."

"If it's true, if Kane's the father, then Noah's safe," Caleb reassured her.

"But he's a monster. Who knows what he's truly capable of?"

"His company ranks are filled with relatives. I read somewhere that he's devoted to family. Noah's his only child. He'd want to keep him close, but he wouldn't hurt his own son."

"No. He'd just use him as a weapon against me." She released a pained sob but gathered herself quickly.

"This is a game changer. Explains why they didn't kill Noah when they didn't get the file." Anger pierced Caleb for not being able to shield her from pain. "The coworker said she was there that day?"

Matt nodded.

"Then we know it was an accident at least." He turned to Matt. "Wait for me outside?"

"Okay."

He settled Katherine onto the makeshift bed and pressed kisses to her forehead, her eyelids, her chin. He held back the new thought plaguing him. That Kane would realize she would never be able to produce the file, and kill her.

"I'll check the area as Matt leaves. Make sure no one followed him."

Katherine's chest rose on harsh breaths. She nodded.

"I want to give him the CD. See if he can find anything. What do you think?"

Those tormented violet eyes looked up at him. She hesitated. "If you trust him, then I agree."

"Good. Try to get some rest. I'll be right back."

She gazed up at him, confused, tired. "He can't be the father. I'll never see Noah again."

"Don't be afraid. When you close your eyes,

I want you to picture me. I'll protect you." She couldn't possibly know just how much he meant those words.

Caleb met his friend on the porch and closed the door. "We need to come up with a plan. But first, we've had a long couple of days, and we need rest."

"It'll be dark soon. You should be all right for tonight. They will figure out where you are eventually. And they'll come with guns blazing. Make no mistake about it," Matt said.

"I know."

"Then what's the game plan? How do you expect to get out of this alive?"

He could see that his friend was coming from a place of caring. "We'll be ready for them. Tomorrow morning, I want you to tell the men to stay away. Margaret, too. Tell them not to come back to work for a few days. That should give us enough time to handle things. Also, I want to meet with the marshal. First thing before daylight." Caleb held out the CD. "And take a look at this. See if you can find a hidden file, or anything that seems suspicious."

Matt took it and studied the cover for a minute. "What has that woman gotten you into?"

"She didn't." Caleb's jaw muscle tensed. Friend or not, Matt had crossed the line. "Look. My eyes were wide open when I decided to help her. You need to know I plan to see this through no matter what."

"Why? What is she to you?"

"You don't get it." He didn't have a real answer to that question so he said goodbye, checking to make sure no one was in the woods lurking, waiting to make a move. "Keep things quiet tonight. Set up the meeting in the tack room."

Matt agreed before disappearing into the thicket.

Caleb moved inside to find Katherine awake, eyes wide open.

"What did you mean when you said you wouldn't leave the ranch again?"

"Did you get enough to eat? I can open and heat a can of soup." He changed the subject as he lit a Coleman lantern, allowing the soft flame to illuminate the room as the sun retreated, casting a dark shadow to fill the room.

"I'm fine. But you're not thinking straight. I won't let you risk your life for me anymore."

"We going down that path again?" What Matt said must've hurt her feelings. "Matt means well. He doesn't know what he's saying."

"I agree with him. They'll go easy on you. I'll tell everyone I shot Ms. Ranker if I have to." Desperation had the muscles in her face rigid as she stood in front of him, moving closer. A red heat climbed up her neck.

"I can't let you lie." He smiled. "Besides, you're no good at it. And the evidence will clear us."

Defiance shot from her glare. Her stubborn streak reared its head again. "You don't get to decide."

Her gaze was fiery hot. Her body vibrated with intensity as she stalked toward him.

He readied himself for the argument that was sure to come, but she pressed a kiss to his lips instead, shocking the hell out of him. More than his spirits rose.

"There's been enough fighting for one day. I need something else from you."

He locked on to her gaze. "Are you sure this is a good idea?"

"No. Not at all. But I need to do it anyway. I want you. I've never wanted a man more. Do you want me?" She tiptoed up and wrapped her arms around his neck. Her eyes darkened, and she was sexy as hell, gazing up at him. A tear fell onto her cheek.

He kissed it away.

"Sorry. I can't remember the last time I cried."

"Don't be." Caleb knew all about holding in emotion. The way it ate at a person's gut until it felt as though there was no stomach lining left. He dropped his other hand to the small of her back. "There's nothing to be ashamed of."

"I'm being stupid. How could anyone want someone who practically cries all over them?"

"I think it's sweet." Rocking his hips, he pressed his erection against her midsection as he cupped her left breast. Heat shot through his body. "This give you any clue as to the question of whether or not I want you?"

Her face lit up with eagerness, and it nearly did him in. "I need to forget about the danger we're in and the fact Noah's been kidnapped, just for a little while." She snuggled against him, shifting her stance to wrap her arms around his waist.

Her sensuality was going to his head faster than a shot of hard liquor. "Hold on there."

"What? You don't think this is a good idea?"

"No. It's been a while for me. And I want this to last."

"Either way there's far too much material between us," she said, stepping back long enough to shrug out of her shirt.

Sight of the delicately laced bra she wore caused a painful spasm in his groin. The light color an interesting contrast to her golden skin.

A second later her shorts fell to the ground, revealing matching cotton panties. The panties he'd picked out for her. Pink.

She stood there, arms at her sides, allowing him a minute to really look at her. "Do you still want me?"

He swallowed a groan. "You're beautiful. You're also determined to end this before it gets started."

"Not exactly. I want long and slow." She unhooked her bra and let it drop before shimmying out of her panties.

Caleb ate up the space between them in one quick stride. His thumb grazed her nipple. It pebbled under his touch and a blast of heat strained his erection. His body needed release. He needed to be inside her where she was warm and wet, moving in rhythm with him until they both exploded and she lay melted in his arms. He needed Katherine.

"You want help with those?" She motioned toward his T-shirt and jeans with a teasing smile that stirred his heart.

His shirt came off in one quick motion and joined her clothing on the floor. She didn't wait for him to unzip his jeans, she was already there, her hands on his zipper. He aided her in their quick removal along with his boxer shorts.

Her eyes widened when they stopped on his full erection. "I want to feel you inside me."

Caleb nearly lost control right there. He needed to think about something else besides the way her honeyed skin would feel wrapped around him. His passion for her hit heights he'd never known with a woman, and he hadn't even entered her yet.

He picked her up and placed her on the bed

before retrieving a condom from his wallet. His hands shook as he attempted to sheath himself.

"Here. Let me." She placed it on his tip and rolled her hand down the shaft.

His muscles went so rigid he felt like an over-strung cello. "You're sexy…and beautiful."

She lay back, watching him. "Then make love to me."

Her thighs parted and he positioned himself in the V. In one thrust, he drove inside her warmth. She was so wet, he nearly exploded. Her body fit him perfectly.

"More," she said through a ragged breath. She gripped his shoulders.

He wanted to make her scream his name a thousand times as he rocketed her toward the ultimate release.

He tensed and struggled to maintain self-control. Not what he was used to. "Not if you want this to last any longer."

He commanded his hips not to move as she traced her fingers down his arms, then onto his back. Her hands came up and anchored on his shoulders as he lowered his mouth over hers, marking her as his. Her silken lips parted, and his tongue drove into her mouth, tasting her hon-eylike sweetness.

Her fingers skimmed along his spine, setting

little fires everywhere she touched. His skin burned with desire only she could release.

Caleb kissed her hard, claiming her mouth as her tongue moved with his. He lightened the kiss softly, allowing her to be in control and to take whatever she needed from him.

In that moment he belonged to her completely, and for as long as she needed him.

And what did he need?

Every needy grasp of her fingertips…every possessive fleck of her tongue…every blast of heat she sent firing through him….

All of her.

She was every bit the woman capable of unleashing his tightly gripped emotions and sending him soaring.

Her tongue delved into his mouth as her fingernails gripped his bottom and he shuddered inside her.

Tremors moved up and down his spine as he pumped her silky heat.

"Caleb," she breathed his name.

He pressed his mouth to the soft curve of her right breast, taking her pointed peak inside his mouth. Her moan was like pouring gasoline on the fire inside him.

He pumped harder as his own desire blazed through his veins.

Hold on…not yet…

He wanted her to explode in his arms into a thousand fragments of light.

He covered her lips, swallowing her next moan and delved his tongue as he bucked his hips.

"Oh, Caleb…"

She tensed her muscles around his erection, and he could feel her nearing the edge.

He pumped faster…harder…deeper…needing to find her core and tantalize her until the mounting fire inside her detonated.

He teased her nipple between his thumb and forefinger, causing her back to arch. Her chestnut hair blazed across the pillow, her body moved in rhythm with his. Her hips wriggled him deeper inside until he thought he might lose all control. She was on the edge, and he felt it.

Her muscles convulsed, and he thrust deeper, again and again, until he felt her completely come undone in his arms. Only then did he allow himself to think about his own release.

Her tight muscles squeezed around his erection and his body reacted, shivering and quaking. In a sensual burst, he let go. Thundered.

In that instant, there was no Caleb or Katherine. They existed together…as the same person… in one body.…

She felt so right in his arms. Would she stay?

Until tomorrow, a little voice said.

Pain gripped him. He couldn't contain his growing feelings for her. This would be over soon. She would be gone. He most likely would never see her again.

Chapter Twelve

The now familiar sounds of the woods, crickets chirping and insects' wings buzzing, broke through the silence in the room. Katherine's sensitized body tingled as Caleb's warm breath moved across her skin. He'd pulled her in tight against him.

Her rapid breathing eventually eased, becoming slow and steady as it found an even tempo. Her heart beat in perfect harmony with his. Everything about the two of them fit together so perfectly. It was so easy to be with Caleb. Being naked with him felt like the most natural thing in the world. She had no insecurities about her body as she lay there. They were like links in a fence, their bond strengthening the whole.

A dumbstruck thought hit her. Their feelings didn't matter anymore. She had Noah to think about. Or did she? She had no idea if he was hurt, or worse. Did Kane even bother to pick up Noah's medication at the drop spot earlier? Would he keep the boy around if he wasn't useful anymore? Logic told her he would, but her heart feared the worst anyway.

If they did survive this nightmare, would she ever see her nephew again? Wouldn't a father trump an aunt? A rich man like Kane could pull strings to ensure she never saw her Noah again.

She recalled the emotions that had drilled through her when she'd found out she'd be responsible for her baby sister. Jealousy. Bitterness. Resentment. They were not the feelings she had about caring for Noah, but she'd known exactly what she was getting into with him. She was older. Ready.

Even though Caleb would never admit it, he would resent her for strapping him down with a ready-made family. If she survived, all her energy had to go toward getting Noah away from Kane.

"Are you sorry?" He broke through her train of thought.

"No. Not for making love. I figured we had to put this attraction behind us so both of us could concentrate. We'll need all our wits about us tomorrow. It was difficult for either one of us to think clearly before."

"And now?" He eyed her suspiciously.

"Everything's crystal clear."

A dark brow lifted. He propped himself up

on one elbow. His muscular body glowed in the soft light.

A well of need sprung up inside Katherine so fast and so desperately she had to take a second to catch her breath and allow her pulse to return to normal—whatever "normal" was anymore.

"And what does that mean exactly?" he asked, eyeing her intently.

"It's highly improbable that all three of us will come out of this alive. If what you said about Kane is true, then at least Noah will be safe." If she and Caleb did survive, could they become a family? He'd spoken so fondly of Savannah, could he grow to accept Noah, too? No. Caleb loved Savannah because he loved her mother. He didn't have those feelings for Katherine. Did he?

Her mind was really playing tricks on her. No way could he have fallen in love with her in such a short time. As much as she'd like to believe the possibility, her practical mind brought her back to reality. They'd been running for their lives. Dodging bullets. They'd narrowly escaped death. He'd been her knight in shining armor, showing up at a time when she needed him most. Of course she had strong feelings for her cowboy. But she shouldn't confuse gratitude for keeping her alive with real affection.

"If I have anything to say about it we will." The way he set his jaw said he meant every word, too.

Even a superhero had a weakness. What was the chink in Caleb's veneer?

Women in trouble.

She needed him, just as Cissy had.

Maybe that was the connection.

Katherine shut the thoughts out of her mind. She didn't want to compare what she and Caleb had with his relationship to the other woman. She didn't even want to think about him with another woman.

"What's the plan?" she asked, trying to redirect her internal conversation.

"Our best bet is to make contact with the marshal."

"Why do you think we can trust him?"

He shrugged. "A hunch."

"Why not contact the sheriff?"

"He'll probably put me in jail."

She gasped. "Surely he doesn't believe you had anything to do with the murder."

"Knowing Coleman, he'd detain me to keep me safe until this whole thing blows over."

"You think there's a chance this'll just go away?" Unrealistic hope flickered inside her and then vanished.

"No. I think they'll keep coming until we're both dead."

"Then we should leave. Hide. I'll go with you."

His dark brow arched. "Would you?"

"If it meant you'd be safe."

"And then as soon as I turned my back you'd disappear and try to protect Noah. You're always looking out for those around you, but who looks out for you?"

A tear welled in her eye. "I don't need anyone."

He grunted. "Like hell you don't. I never met anyone who needed people more."

Like Cissy?

Why did the admission hurt so much?

His reasons for helping her were becoming transparent. "Does your cowboy code force you to save all damsels in distress?"

His jaw muscles pulsed and his gaze narrowed. Anger radiated from him. "Being with you has nothing to do with obligation."

"Then what?" She hated feeling so insecure and so vulnerable. Maybe that's why she'd spent so much time blocking out the world? Considering Caleb was about the only true friend she had and they'd just met. She'd been doing a great job of keeping people away to date. Didn't everyone let her down eventually?

He didn't immediately answer.

"I was doing fine by myself before you came along," she lied. She told herself if she could close her eyes, she might even be able to rest.

He pressed a kiss to her forehead. "I know you

were. But I wasn't. And I don't know what I'd do without you here."

The thin layer of ice protecting her heart from being broken melted. "We might never know why he's after us." She fell silent. The rock of dread positioned on her chest grew heavier. Her chest walls felt as though they were caving in…as if she was drowning and couldn't get air into her lungs. Leann's secret was a boulder tied around Katherine's neck as she catapulted to the ocean floor.

"Maybe Matt will see something on the CD we overlooked. We didn't exactly have time to dig around on it before they caught up to us," Caleb offered.

"You're sure we can trust him?"

"I'd put my life in his hands."

He just did. And hers, too. Matt didn't hide the fact he didn't have the same dedication to Katherine that he did to Caleb. At least she knew exactly where she stood with him. "He doesn't think you should be around me."

"Just proves he doesn't know what's best for me."

"I can't see a way out of this. Even if you talk to the marshal, you're taking a risk. He might be on Kane's payroll. How can we know he'll be of assistance to us?"

Caleb shrugged his shoulders. The light from

the lantern made his face look even more handsome. "Don't see another choice."

"Me, either. You're right. We need help from someone."

"I can leave before the sun comes up to get Matt. I'll be back before the first light with a few answers. For now, I'd like to try to sleep. Unless you can think of something better to do." He quirked a devastating grin.

One look was all it took for him to stir her sexually. "As a matter of fact, I can. And I think we make love quite well."

"All the more reason for us to keep doing it," he said with one of his trademark looks.

"Unless you're too tired." She repositioned herself better to kiss him, enjoying the feel of the perfect fit of their naked bodies. His was like pure silk over finely tuned muscle.

"Are you doubting me?"

She kissed his collarbone. "That wouldn't be a wise move on my part. I've seen your stamina. But even you have to sleep sometime."

"After a while," he said, pressing his erection to her thigh. "Right now, I have something else demanding attention."

This time, their lovemaking was slow and tender. Did they both realize each moment together was a precious gift to be savored and enjoyed?

CALEB ROSE BEFORE the sun and heated water for coffee while Katherine slept. He'd had to force himself away from her to get out of bed. Every bone in his body wanted to curl up with her, hold her. He hadn't wanted to leave a second before he had to. He'd managed a few hours of shut-eye, thanks to her being by his side.

He'd expected coming back to the homestead would evoke a hailstorm of bad memories. It didn't.

Katherine had chased away those demons for him, he thought while he let Max outside to take care of his business.

Caleb kept the door cracked open as he opened a can of beef stew and heated it for the pint-size critter. The little guy had been too stressed to eat last night. He'd curled in the corner and slept until he heard Caleb stir. His little ears had perked up and he'd whined until Caleb went to get him.

Time seemed to drip by as Caleb glanced at his watch for the third time in five minutes. Matt was supposed to meet him in the tack room, providing it was safe. He'd been tasked with making contact with the marshal, and trying to figure out what Caleb had missed on the CD.

The unanswered questions in this case weren't helping matters. If he knew what information Kane was looking for, he could provide a better bluff.

One wrong move and boom.

Caleb had not expected to let himself get involved with another woman so quickly. Hell, he was beginning to doubt if he'd ever find true love. What he'd had with Cissy couldn't be classified as such. Real love meant putting others before yourself.

He'd told himself his entire life he hadn't gotten involved with a woman because of his devotion to making a success out of his life.

Was it?

He'd almost made a full-time job of avoiding relationships, hadn't he?

And how much of it had to do with your screwed-up childhood?

In trying to avoid being like his father, had he closed the door to finding anything real in his life?

He'd told himself he didn't have time for women, that all he could afford to focus on was work in order to have a better life. Money didn't buy happiness, but being poor didn't, either. He'd had a ringside seat to that show throughout his childhood.

If his mother could have afforded insurance, she would have been able to take better care of herself.

If his old man had stuck around, she wouldn't have had to be the sole provider.

If they'd had more money, she wouldn't have had to work so hard.

If. If. If.

Was he the one to blame for his relationships not working out? For Cissy? He could tell himself she'd used him till the cows came home, but had he given her anything to hang on to?

He had his doubts.

All his heartache, all his loving memories, had little to do with her and everything to do with the thought of having a real family. His heart ached for the idea of a family, not his ex-girlfriend. And why didn't he really miss her? Or any of the other dozen women he'd spent time with in the past?

Is it because they weren't Katherine Harper? asked a quiet voice from the back of his mind.

Whether he wanted to acknowledge it or not, if anything happened to her, he would never be the same again.

Chapter Thirteen

Katherine couldn't remember the last time she'd slept so deeply. Dangerous under the circumstances. Caleb's outdoorsy and masculine scent was all over her...the sheets...bringing out a sensual daydream.

She got out of bed, needing to leave this room, this place, as fast as she could. She felt stifled being on his property, in his homestead with reminders of him everywhere, knowing it wouldn't last.

Her ankle tolerated some weight as she hobbled into the makeshift kitchen trying not to think about Caleb's absence.

The possibility he might not come back crossed her mind. Then what?

They hadn't discussed a contingency plan for that.

Katherine struck the thought from her mind. Caleb would return. They would figure out an arrangement. Somehow, some way, they would find a way out of this mess.

She thought about Leann, wondering if her sister had believed the same thing when she'd decided to take these men on by herself.

What file did Leann have that would make Kane turn on her family?

Did she have any idea what she was up against? Did Katherine?

Kane's twenty-four-hour deadline to produce the file had come and gone. His men were out there, searching for her, ready and waiting. Something told her they'd never give up until she was dead, file or not.

Caleb was out there somewhere, too, putting himself in harm's way for her again. He'd promised to be back before she woke, before sunrise, and yet the sun was blazing in the east. A little piece of her heart died at the thought of anything happening to him.

She stopped at the door and her gaze went to the bed. They'd made love right there last night again and again until their bodies were zapped of strength and they gave in to sleep.

Being near him had made her feel more connected to him than anyone else on the planet. They'd made love intensely, sweetly, passionately, until their bodies became entwined and she could no longer tell where he stopped and she began.

They became one body, one being.

The idea of losing him, losing one more person she loved, was worse than a dagger through the chest.

She sat on the floor, stroking Max's neck absently. The strong coffee revived her. She redressed the wounds on her leg. Some of the gashes were deeper than others but they all looked to be healing rather quickly given the circumstances. The swelling was going down on her ankle. A few more days of rest and she'd be all better.

The external wounds would heal. As for the internal damage, that would depend on how the events of the day progressed.

She sighed deeply. Where was Caleb?

CALEB DIDN'T LIKE the idea of leaving Katherine alone all morning. Matt had been late and that had pushed back the whole morning's timeline.

During the meeting, all Caleb's danger radar fired on high alert. He couldn't figure out if it was because of the marshal or because he'd left Katherine alone in the homestead unguarded.

The meeting with the marshal ran over and Caleb's pulse hammered every extra second he was there. This whole scenario could be a scam to get Katherine alone. That's exactly what the marshal would do if he was on Kane's payroll.

Matt hadn't found any secret files, either, not that he was a computer guru. Caleb needed to talk to Katherine about handing it over to the marshal. The government would have the necessary resources available to uncover anything on the CD. Problem was, they'd have to be able to trust the Feds first. If there was a leak in the department, turning over evidence could be more than a huge mistake. It could be a fatal one.

The idea burned Caleb's gut. He couldn't decide if he wanted to put these guys behind bars or take them out himself. The idea they would threaten an innocent child to get to Katherine fired instant rage in his belly.

There were too many "ifs" to feel good about a decision one way or the other.

He wouldn't make a call without filling her in first.

Climbing onto the porch step, the knot in his gut tightened. Maybe he should've taken her with him and stashed her somewhere close by during the meeting.

No. She was safest right where she was and a part of him knew it. Damn that he was second-guessing himself.

Maybe it was because of the news he had to deliver. Or that a little voice kept reminding him she would leave him. If not now, then later.

Relief hit him faster than a rain shower in a drought when he stepped inside and saw her on the floor playing with Max.

Her eyes were wide. "Thank God. You're all right."

He moved to her and pressed kisses to her temples. "Matt was late. He thought someone might be following him. I'm sorry you were worried."

"How'd it go?"

"He didn't find anything on the CD. The marshal might be able to if we give him access."

She moved to the counter and then handed him a tin cup filled with coffee. "I can't decide. What's your first instinct?"

"The government can hack into just about anything." He took the disk from his pocket and held it out between them. "If we can trust the bastards, they'll find what we're looking for."

She palmed it. "What if there's nothing on it?"

"We'll have to cross that bridge when we come to it." He paused a beat. "Even if there's enough evidence on this to lock him away forever, there's something else you should know."

Her violet eyes were enormous. "You're scaring me."

"The marshal said Kane has most likely left the United States."

She sat there, looking dumbfounded. "How can that be?"

"It's believed he has a compound across the border in Mexico. The marshal is working on a few leads, gathering more intel."

"What's the use of turning over the CD when everyone, including me, will be dead before they capture him?"

Not if Caleb had anything to say about it. "I know how hopeless this feels."

"Why does he even need the file when he can disappear out of the country with Noah?" She stared blankly at the door. "And I suppose we're just supposed to let the government take its sweet time finding Kane? Meanwhile, he has an assault squad on us."

"They've offered protection."

She blew out a breath. "Like that would do any good. They'd find us eventually."

"Maybe not."

Silence sat between them for a long beat. "I would never see Noah again."

"That's not going to happen."

"Did he say what Kane is after?"

"Said Leann has evidence linking him to a crime."

"I know I haven't painted a great picture of my sister. But she was a good person. I can't imagine why she would get involved with a man like that."

"The marshal said she didn't know. She was young when they met. He swept her off her feet.

Spent lots of money on her. He was a successful businessman. Everything looked legit. By the time she figured out his dark side, she was pregnant. She disappeared and had her baby. Never planned to tell him he was the father. Kept the evidence of his crime stashed away just in case he showed up again. And then, one day, he walked into the coffee shop. There she was. She pretended that she missed him and secretly got in touch with the Feds. She was planning to turn state's evidence to keep him away from Noah."

"Explains why she moved around so much before. With Noah getting close to school age, she wanted to put down roots. Do they know what evidence she had against him?"

"She offered to provide pictures to back up her testimony." He issued a grunt. "I think you should take the deal. Let them tuck you away somewhere safe."

"They'll kill Noah."

"Kane won't hurt his son."

"How am I supposed to do that?" Her response was rapid, shooting flames of accusation.

"It'll keep you alive until they can find Kane and Noah."

"And then what? Live out the rest of my life in fear? Alone? Waiting for him to finally figure out where I am? He won't stop until he finds me. I don't know where the picture is. I can't put him away without it. If this guy is as ruthless as they say, Kane won't let up until I'm dead."

She had a good point and Caleb knew it. "It's just an option."

"And what about you, Caleb? Where will you go?"

"I already said it once. I won't leave my ranch."

An incredulous look crossed her features. "They'll find you and kill you. They won't even have to look far."

"I'll be fine. You're not thinking straight."

"Oh, so what am I now? A crazy lunatic? Can you look me in the eyes and tell me I'm wrong?"

He lowered his gaze. "No."

"What's your plan?"

"I'm going to stay and fight. No matter how many men they send, I'll return them in body bags if I have to," he said, determination welling in his chest.

"I shouldn't have to run and hide. I didn't do anything wrong," she said, pacing.

"They'll use Noah as bait to get to you. And you to get to me. You know that, right?"

"Let them. It's obvious they won't let up until I'm dead or Kane's locked away. I may not be able to change the cards I was dealt, but I can decide how to play them."

Her stubborn streak was infuriating. And damn sexy.

"I hear what you're saying, but if anything happens to you, it's game over. At least with you alive, we have cards left to play. He will have a lingering doubt about the file. He'll have no choice but to hide." Couldn't she see he was trying to save her? Why did she have to be so stubborn?

You'd be the same way, a distant voice said.

Her chin jutted out. "I thought last night meant something. Why would you want me to disappear from your life forever?"

With every part of him, he didn't. But he'd say anything if it meant keeping her safe. "We got caught up in the moment. I think you should go." Damn but it nearly killed him to say those words.

The pure look of hurt in her eyes nearly made him take it back. He couldn't. He wouldn't let her stick around because of him. He told himself she'd be safer in custody.

"Then I will leave. But I'll be damned if you get to tell me where I'll go." Her lips quivered but she didn't cry.

He'd seen that same look of bravery on her how many times now and it still had the same effect on him.

She grabbed her bag and made a start for the door.

Caleb stepped in front of her, blocking passage. "Where exactly are you going?"

"I don't know and you shouldn't care." Katherine was a study in determination.

KATHERINE'S HEART HAD been ripped from her chest. She knew whatever she and Caleb had couldn't last, and yet his words harpooned her. "Get out of my way, I have something to do."

"I shouldn't have pushed you away. I'm sorry. I only said those things because I thought they might influence you to go into protective custody. I didn't mean a word of it. It's killing me that I can't protect you."

Was he lying then or now?

Katherine had no idea. Everything in her heart wanted to believe this was the truth. That whatever they had between them was genuine and real. The physical attraction had to be, she reasoned. No one could fake what had happened between them last night that convincingly. The sex had been complete rapture. No other man had made her feel like that—sexy, beautiful, devoured. He'd drank in every last inch of her and come back for more. Everything about the night was still vivid in her mind. His gorgeous body, bathed in moonlight and the soft glow of the lantern. His cinnamon taste that was still on her lips.

When he'd entered her, she'd felt on top of the world, as though she was soaring above the earth and didn't need air to breathe. She'd felt more alive in that moment than she had her entire life.

Then again, maybe it was purely physical for him.

Sex for sex's sake.

Didn't men view intimacy differently than women?

Maybe the whole experience was food for his sexual appetite. A man like Caleb was surely used to having his way with women. One look at him, his honey-gold skin and brown eyes with their gold flecks, would stir any woman who could see.

The sex had probably been far more special to her than him. Or maybe she refused to acknowledge the possibility he'd love her and could accept her nephew as his own someday. And she would get Noah back.

"I'd like you to move," she said, tears welling in her eyes.

He didn't budge. Instead he stared at her incredulously.

"Now." How dare he? Hadn't he just told her she meant nothing to him? And now he had the audacity to pretend to care.

"I'm not going anywhere until you believe me."

"Then we'll be here all day."

"I can think of a good way to spend 'all day' here." He got that mischievous look in his eye. The reminder he knew how to take what he wanted.

Katherine's thin veneer was cracking. She folded her arms. "Let me go."

"What's the matter? Afraid you'll run out of excuses to push me away?" He broadened his stance and quirked a devastating smile.

Damn. He knew he was getting to her.

Her hands came up to his chest again to push him away, but he stepped toward her and she ended up gripping his shoulders to steady herself from the physical force that was all Caleb.

Tension crackled in the air between them as he stared at her, his gaze filled with desire. He leaned down and kissed her so tenderly it robbed her ability to breathe.

"I'm sorry I said those things to you. I was a jerk."

The crack expanded like ice defrosting.

"Yes. You were." She leaned into his broad chest.

"Can you forgive me?"

Katherine was startled to realize there wasn't much he could do she wouldn't forgive.

Not that it mattered. Pretty soon, she'd be exactly where Kane wanted her.

Chapter Fourteen

"We need to make contact with Marshal Jones. See if we have anything to work with here." Caleb pointed to the CD.

"How do we do that?"

"Jones gave me this." Caleb pulled a cell from his pocket and held it out. "It's secure."

"Must be. No one has showed up with a gun," she said.

He opened the contacts, touched the name Marshal Jones and then the call button. "Katherine is willing to turn over the CD we discussed," Caleb said, a little weary they were about to hand over their best and only playing card. "But I need some reassurances."

"I'll go with an outside guy to examine it. No one else will see it," Jones said, answering the un-asked question.

"I like where you're headed. Go on."

"Served with him in Iraq. He was dishonorably discharged when he punched his sergeant for his stupidity. Let's just say there's no love lost between this guy and the government."

That's exactly what Caleb wanted to hear. "Then he sounds perfect for the job."

"He will be. If there's anything on the CD, you'll know it. We'll catch up to Kane eventually. And we'll have the evidence ready when we do."

Caleb caught Katherine flexing her hands. Was she trying to stop them from shaking? Was she still angry about his harsh words?

He picked up Max and pointed to a wooden chair. When she sat, he handed her the little mutt. The best way to lower her blood pressure was to get her interacting with the dog. It might distract her enough to calm her down. Give her time to think through his actions—actions that would convince her his feelings were real.

"And until then?"

"We need to keep searching. He'll make a mistake, and we'll be there to catch him. He'll know anything we do is most likely a trap. He could just send his minions to do his dirty work, and I can't guarantee anyone's safety if you're not in custody," Jones said.

Caleb walked outside onto the porch. "He'll come for us. This is personal. He'd never planned to hurt his own son. It's always been about taking back evidence and silencing Katherine."

"You may be right. Don't take any chances. I can order extra security."

"Matt will insist on helping, too."

"I don't want to risk any more civilian lives, but I won't stop you. I'll speak to Sheriff Coleman, too. He might be able to provide some assistance. We'll cover all the bases we can," Jones said ominously.

"I feel a lot more comfortable with the odds of keeping her safe at the ranch. It's better than being out there where anything can happen. I can control who has access to the main house. I'll take her there as soon as it's dark. Don't want to move around during the day if I don't have to."

"I'll have the results by morning. If I find what I'm looking for on that CD, we'll arrest him the minute he shows his face in the U.S. again."

"And her nephew?"

"He'll go back to his aunt where he belongs."

"Other than your men, I don't want anyone else knowing we're staying at the ranch," Caleb insisted.

"Agreed. There's no sense inviting more trouble than we already have coming to this party. We'll have our hands full as it is. No additional government agency involvement apart from my men and Coleman. Your location is easy to secure by vehicle with only one road in and out. I'll station someone near the main house and another officer at the mouth of the drive."

"I'll turn over the CD to the officer on duty." Caleb closed the cell, walked back inside and filled Katherine in on the part of the conversation she missed.

Katherine's body language was easy to read. She was curled up with Max in her lap, making herself as small as she could possibly become. She wanted to disappear.

It wasn't cold inside the homestead, but she was shivering slightly. No doubt, she wanted to block out everything that was happening to her.

"It'll be nice for you to sleep in your own bed for a change," Katherine mused, doing her level best to steer the conversation away from anything stressful. She knew on some level that Caleb hadn't meant to hurt her, but her wounds were still fresh. She needed a minute. Something told her Kane was close by. A man like him would want to finish what he started. No chance he'd walk away and leave her alone.

"No argument there. Except I'll give you the soft bed to sleep on while I keep watch." Caleb moved to the food supplies and opened a can of beans. When they were warm, he offered her first dibs.

"No thanks. I ate a protein bar that was stashed

here." The ticking clock was a reminder of how little time she had left. How little time either of them had left. "Did Marshal Jones mention anything about Noah?"

Caleb shook his head.

The pressure was stringing her nerves too tight. A half-desperate laugh slipped out. "I'll just keep hoping for the best then."

He moved to her and kissed her. Warmly. She didn't resist. He tasted like coffee.

"Do you want me to make some more of Margaret's calming tea?" he asked with a wink.

She straightened her shoulders. "God, no. I'm a coffee person through and through."

A white-toothed smile broke across Caleb's face. "You really are determined to hold it together, aren't you?"

"Not on the inside. I'm a wreck." That much was true.

"I'd never be able to tell." He kissed her again.

He pulled her down on his lap as he sat, embracing her as though he might never see her again. He held her as though one of them could be gone tomorrow. Or both.

The gravity of what they were facing hit her hard.

A wave of melancholy washed over her. She'd been so intent on finding a way to bring Kane out into the open, she hadn't really considered the position she was putting herself in or the consequences. "Promise me that if something happens to me, you'll find Noah anyway and get him away from that animal."

His grip tightened around her as his breath warmed her neck. "Don't have to. You'll be around to take care of him yourself."

She turned enough to look into his brown eyes. "Promise me anyway."

His expression was a mix of sadness, regret and sheer grit. "I will not let anything happen to you. That much I can vow."

She could tell from the intensity in his gaze he would take a bullet for her if that was the only way to protect her.

"Drink up." He motioned to her cup. "It'll be dark outside soon. In a short while we can shower and eat a real meal at the main house."

"Both sound almost too good to be true. Although I haven't exactly felt like I've been suffering out here. Not compared to what we've been through." Or the hell she faced at the thought of never seeing Noah again.

Caleb smiled his trademark smile. He rose, let Max out and stood at the open door.

She brought her hand up to his neck. If they survived this ordeal, could the three of them think about a future together? Would he resent having a ready-made family as she had all those years ago?

Or could he love Noah the same way he did Savannah?

CALEB COULDN'T SEE. He didn't have time to let his eyes adjust, either. He knew this trail better than the back of his hand. The path from the homestead to the ranch was thick with trees. They provided much-needed shelter from a sweltering August sun and would afford cover for them now.

He fumbled for Katherine's hand and then slipped through the mesquites in the black, moonless night.

Quietly he made his way through the woods he loved so much. Every tree, every stream, felt so much like a part of him, entwined with his soul. He'd memorized and mentally mapped every inch of his property.

Once inside the house, Caleb bolted the lock. Not that it would do much good against the kind of firepower Kane's men would bring to the fight, but it would make Katherine feel better.

Keeping her as calm and relaxed as he could under the circumstances became his marching orders. "Which sounds better right now—a hot shower or a good meal while I take the CD to Jones's guy out front?"

She sighed. "I'll take either. Both. But let me take one more look at that before we turn it over."

"You know where the office is. Password is Tor-Jake." He handed her a couple ibuprofen and a bottle of water, shoving the fear he could lose her down deep. "Then you get cleaned up while I see what's in the fridge."

"Deal." She popped the pills in her mouth and downed them with a gulp of water before disappearing down the hall with the disk.

He showered and brushed his teeth in the guest room before returning to the kitchen. The CD sat on the counter near the coffeepot. He could hear the shower going in the master bathroom.

Caleb trucked outside and waved as he neared the cruiser. "Marshal Jones is expecting this. Said you'd know what to do with it."

"Yes, sir," the officer said, opening the door. When he stood, he wasn't more than five foot ten but had a stocky build. "I'll take it to him. There's an officer stationed at the top of the road. He'll keep watch until I return."

Caleb thanked him and returned to the house.

Margaret had stacked several Tupperware containers filled with food in the fridge with a note on top. "This should keep you from getting too skinny until I get back in a couple of days."

The idea of eating Margaret's food was almost enough to bring a smile to his lips again. She'd made several of his favorite meals. There was a roast with those slow-cooked rosemary potatoes he loved, a tub full of sausage manicotti, and what looked like smoked brisket. There were mashed potatoes in another container and some greens.

Caleb pulled out the roast, fixed two plates and heated them in the microwave.

Katherine stepped into the kitchen wearing one of his T-shirts and a pair of shorts. Seeing her in his clothes, in his house, stirred his heart. God, he needed her.

She was as beautiful as looking at the endless sky on a clear blue day.

He didn't want this moment to end. For them to end. An ominous feeling it wouldn't last plagued him.

She walked over to him, inclined her head and pressed those sweet lips to his.

The second the kiss deepened, Caleb lifted Katherine and carried her to the bedroom, shooing Max away with his foot.

He made love to her so completely, so thoroughly, she fell asleep in his arms. Right where she belonged.

Chapter Fifteen

Caleb's body warmed Katherine's back. Forget sleep tonight. Her leg hurt. Her throat was dry.

Could she move without waking him?

Even if she managed to slip out of bed undetected, there was Max to deal with. Her nerves were banded so tight, she felt as though one might snap.

Slowly, she rolled away from him until she could feel the edge of the bed. The absence of his touch made her skin cold and her heart ache. She ignored the painful stabs in her chest and slipped off the bed.

Thankfully, Max didn't make a sound. It was too dark to see him, but she figured he was sleeping at the foot of the bed.

She tiptoed out of the room. She'd hoped to feel some relief when they'd come back to the ranch. Instead, the hairs on her neck prickled.

Something brushed against her leg. A yelp escaped before she could suppress it.

Claws?

Katherine squinted. Light streamed in from the window in the hallway. "Here, kitty."

Claws stalked away without looking back.

The kitchen was dark save for the light coming in through the window.

She checked the clock and calculated it had been at least four hours since her last dose of pain medication. She palmed a couple of ibuprofen. Turning the spigot, she scanned the yard.

Where was the officer? His sedan was there. Parked. Doors open. Lights on.

Ice trickled down her spine.

She shook it off.

An officer was parked at the top of the lane and another was right outside the door. It was safe here.

She downed the contents of her glass and set it on the sink.

Where was the officer? If he was walking the perimeter, wouldn't he close the door?

She peeked out the screen door. Nothing stuck out as odd.

The crackle of a radio broke through. She stepped out onto the porch. Outside, every chirp seemed amplified.

The pain in her ankle flared despite the compression sock.

She limped to the edge of the porch. Her mind clicked through a few possibilities. Was the other officer at his post?

Maybe they'd met somewhere in the middle?

Her warning systems flared. She should probably turn and run back into the house. Wake Caleb.

"Anyone here?" she whispered.

The place was quiet. She said a silent protection prayer. Her heart thumped in her throat. Her mouth was so dry she couldn't manage enough spit to swallow.

She checked around the corner.

Nothing.

No one.

Frustration impaled her. Caleb needed sleep. Surely the officer was fine.

It might be a false alarm, but better safe than sorry.

She turned to the back door. Before she could hit her stride, a strong hand crashed down on her shoulder, knocking her backward. The icy fingers were like a vise. She tried to scream. A hand covered her mouth.

"I don't think so, honey," said the male voice.

She recognized it immediately. Scarface.

Using all the force she had, Katherine kicked and threw her elbows into him to break free.

A blast of cold metal hit the back of her head. Blackness.

WAKING TO FIND Katherine out of bed had disturbed Caleb. He'd already checked the house. Hadn't found her. Desperation railed through him. She wouldn't leave him. Would she?

He checked outside.

The officer wasn't at his post, either.

Noise came from the barn before Caleb reached the doors. His stallion was kicking and snorting.

What had Samson riled up?

Caleb didn't like it.

Then again, there wasn't anything about this situation he remotely *liked* so far. The caution bells sounded louder the closer he got to the barn until he couldn't hear his own thoughts anymore.

Katherine was in grave danger. He could feel it in every one of his bones. He sent a text to Marshal Jones. What had happened to his men?

The closer Caleb moved toward Samson, the more intense his fears became.

Caleb slowed his pace, his steps steady, deliberate. "Whoa, boy."

Katherine was missing. His chest nearly caved in at the thought. *Kane.*

His next call was to his friend.

Matt picked up on the first ring.

Caleb let out the breath he'd been holding. "Katherine's gone. I think Kane has her."

"Damn. What do you need me to do?"

"Where are you?"

"Dallas. At the hospital with Jimmy."

"I don't know," Caleb lowered his tone.

From the north side of the woods, a tall man stalked toward him.

"I gotta go. Don't worry about being here," Caleb said, ending the call.

The guy was big, but Caleb had no doubt he could take him down if need be. As he moved into the light, he recognized Marshal Jones.

"Where are your men?"

"Sent one of my guys to deliver the CD. I've been trying to reach the other stationed at the top of the drive with no luck. I wanted to be close by so I parked up the road in the woods."

"Kane's here. It's the only explanation." Caleb glanced at his watch. "I don't know when he got to her." It could have been hours ago.

"My man was here fifteen minutes ago. They can't have gotten far. I'll radio again. There's no other way out of here by car, is there?" Jones fell into step with Caleb, who pointed his flashlight at the ground.

"One road in. One road out. There's countless ways to reach the house through the woods. None of which a car would fit through." Caleb glanced up. "Think they got to your guy?"

"Must've. He would answer his radio otherwise."

"Bastards." The white dot illuminated the

yellow-green grass as Caleb moved closer to the tree line. "They used ATVs before. They're smart. They've studied the terrain."

He trained his flashlight on a spot on the ground.

"Hold on." He dropped to his knees.

"A woman's footprint."

"It's hers." He shone the light east. "The footprint stops here." He glanced around on the ground. "See that?"

"A man's shoe print."

"Which means someone carried her." Caleb followed the imprints to the tree line. "They went this way."

"They most likely have a car stashed somewhere," Jones said as he turned toward the lane. "I'll head to the main road."

"You said you heard from one of your guys fifteen minutes ago?"

"Yes."

"It would take about that long to run to the nearest place they could've hid a car. You take the road." Caleb ran toward the barn. "I can cut them off on horseback."

KATHERINE'S EYES BLURRED as she tried to blink them open. The crown of her head felt as though someone had blasted her with a hammer. Her thoughts jumbled. Thinking clearly through her pounding headache would be a challenge.

In a flash, she remembered being outside before someone grabbed her and then the lights went out. Didn't seem like anyone had turned them back on, either. Pitch-black wasn't nearly good enough to describe the darkness surrounding her. Where was she? Where was Caleb? Terror gripped her.

Chill bumps covered her arms. She reached out and hit surface in every direction without extending her arms. Was she in some kind of compartment? Whatever she was in moved fast. She bounced, bumping her head.

She lay on a clothlike material. The whole area couldn't measure more than three or four feet deep and she couldn't stretch out her legs.

Realization dawned. Icy fingers of panic gripped her lungs and squeezed.

She was in the trunk of a car.

Oh, God. How would she get out? Wasn't there a panic lever somewhere?

At least her arms and legs were free. She felt around for something—anything—to pop the trunk. Was there a weapon? A car jack?

Her mind cleared and she recalled more details. Scarface's voice.

Katherine listened carefully to the sounds around her. The engine revved. Brakes squealed as the car flew side to side.

A thump sounded. A gunshot rang out.

Her throat closed as fear seized her.

The car roared to a stop.

She repositioned herself so her feet faced the lid. She'd be ready to launch an attack at whoever opened the trunk.

Her heart hammered in her chest. She held her breath, fighting off sheer terror. *Patience.*

The trunk lid lifted and she thrust her feet at the body leaning toward her. She made contact at the same time she recognized the face. "Caleb?"

His arms reached for her, encircled her, while her brain tried to catch up. He lifted her and carried her to his horse.

His face was a study in concentration and determination. He didn't speak as he balanced her in his arms and popped her into the saddle. He hopped up from behind just in time for her to see that his jeans were soaked with blood on his right thigh. Her heart skipped a beat. She told herself he'd be fine. He had to be okay. His arms circled her as he gripped the reins.

Scarface hadn't fared so well. He was slumped over the steering wheel. "Is he dead?"

"No." Caleb urged his horse forward as lights and sirens wailed from behind. "But he'll wish he was after the marshal gets hold of him."

The feel of Caleb against her back, warming

her, brought a sense of rightness to the crazy world. "You found me."

She could feel every muscle in his chest tense.

Samson kept a steady gallop until they reached the barn. Caleb took care of his horse, then, keeping Katherine by his side, headed for the house.

"I walked outside to check on the officer. I turned around to come get you when I heard his voice. Then everything went black. I'm so sorry."

"Don't be. I'm just glad I found you." He pressed kisses to her forehead, then her nose before feathering them on her cheeks. "I can't lose you."

His lips pressed to hers with bruising need.

She loved him. There was no questioning that. But what was he offering? A commitment? Her heart gave a little skip at the thought. He'd already proved he would be there for her no matter what. When the chips were down, he'd come through for her, comforting her, saving her. He was the one person in the world she trusted. "I heard a gunshot and panicked. What happened while I was in the trunk?"

"Scarface took aim. There were too many twists in the road for him to be able to steer and shoot, or…"

"Oh, God. Did he hit you?" She scanned his jeans for a bullet hole, panicked when she noticed the blood.

"Grazed my leg. Flesh wound. I'm fine. I caught up to him before he got off another round."

She couldn't hold back the sob that broke free. She couldn't even think about something happening to Caleb.

"I'm okay. I promise."

She buried her face in his chest, her body shaking. His arms tightened around her.

"Let's get you inside."

"We should get back on the road. Follow Scarface. Maybe he can lead us to Noah?"

"I doubt it. Scarface should be in custody by now. Unless the marshal let him go to follow him. Putting yourself in danger again won't help that little boy."

"This isn't about him anymore, is it?" A chill ran down her spine at the realization. "Kane is after me now."

"For his own freedom. He wants to erase you and the file." Caleb's gaze scanned the trees. "Let's get you inside."

CALEB CLEANED HIS injuries. He dabbed water on his leg, thinking how much he needed to keep his head clear. He dressed the cut on his thigh and changed into clean jeans.

"They might be out there right now," Katherine said as she sat down on his bed. "That's what you were just thinking, wasn't it?"

"Yes."

She glanced at the windows, her tentative smile replaced by a look of apprehension. "What do we do now?"

"I'll reconnect with the marshal and then go after the son of a bitch as soon as we figure out the next step. Until then, we wait here. I won't let him hurt the woman I love again."

"Love?" She rewarded him with a smile. "I love you, too."

BY THE TIME Matt eased in the back door, Katherine's nerves were sizzling. "I thought you were in Dallas."

"Came back to help you."

"Why would you do that?"

"When Caleb said he'd found you, I came to stop them from doing anything else." He excused himself, saying he needed to find Caleb.

She made a pot of coffee in the dim light, having allowed her eyes to adjust to the darkness, surprised Matt would want to come to her aid. She glanced out the window. Were they out there watching? Who else would Kane send?

They could be anywhere right now. Even standing outside, looking right at her. A chill ran up her spine. She had to figure out a way to get Caleb to let her come with him to find Kane.

A noise from behind shattered what was left of

her brittle nerves. She turned to find Matt standing there. Her hand came up to her chest.

"Didn't mean to scare you," he said.

"It's fine. I'm jumpy." She held up a mug. "Coffee?"

"I can get it. You should sit down. Caleb said you have to be careful on that ankle."

"Believe it or not, it was much worse yesterday." She eyed him warily. He looked determined to say something. She filled a mug and handed it to him. "How about I let you get your own cream and sugar?"

"I take mine black."

There was another thing to like about him. Under ordinary circumstances, she figured they might actually get along. She reminded herself they weren't really friends and he likely hadn't sought her out to talk about the coffee.

"Me, too," she said anyway, figuring he also didn't want to hear about how much they had in common—such as how much they both cared for Caleb. But that was another common bond between them, whether Matt like it or not.

"I'm not good at this sort of thing…." He paused.

She took a sip, welcoming the burn and the warmth on her throat.

Another beat passed as he shifted his weight onto his other foot.

Whatever he had to say, Katherine figured she wasn't about to be showered with compliments. She braced herself for what would come next. She'd stared down worse bulls than a protective friend.

Didn't he realize she had Caleb's best interests at heart?

When he looked as though saying the words out loud might actually cause him physical pain, she said, "I can save you the trouble. I know you don't like me. But if you gave me half a chance, I think we could be friends."

There. She'd said it. She put it out there between them, and he could do what he wanted with it.

She crossed her arms and readied herself for his response.

"That isn't what I came here to say."

"Okay."

"I need to apologize."

"No, you don't." The tension in her neck muscles eased.

His stance was firm and unmoving. "I appreciate you saying that, but I do."

"If the tables were turned and it was me, I'd probably feel the same way as you. I can see how this looks. A stranger shows up on his property and he puts his life in danger to help her. I wouldn't like it, either."

The corner on one side of his mouth lifted. "There is that."

"You must love him a lot."

"Like the brother I never had."

"But I do, too." Had she just admitted her true feelings for Caleb to the one man who could stand her the least? It was one thing to say it to Caleb. Damn. It had come out so fast and yet sounded so natural. Felt natural. Her heart was so full it might burst that he'd said it to her first. But to make the declaration to a friend? To let everyone else know took the relationship to a new level. Was she ready?

Katherine steadied her nerves. Her admission would probably spark a rebellion anyway. Why couldn't she just leave it alone? Why did she need Matt to understand her feelings for Caleb?

Because Matt was like family to him. He was important.

She secretly wished for his approval.

"I know," Matt said softly. "He feels the same way. I knew it the first time I saw him with you."

Katherine stood stunned. "I had no idea."

"It's half the reason I've been so…worried," Matt said, leaning against the counter.

"I realize you know him best. You must've seen that look before?"

"No. Never. Not with anyone else." His tone was deadpan.

Katherine's heart skipped a beat. Maybe she could believe his love was real. He wasn't confusing his need to help with true feelings. Maybe this was different than the women in his past.

Caleb strolled in before she could thank Matt for telling her. "Not with any what?"

Chapter Sixteen

Katherine held out a mug. "Coffee's fresh."

Caleb arched his brow. The corners of his lips turned up and he winked. He walked to her and wrapped his arms around her waist. "You're not getting out of this so easy. What were the two of you talking about?"

Matt made an excuse about walking the perimeter and slipped outside.

"I remembered something that might help. I'd completely forgotten about Leann's phone. I can contact Kane if we can get another power cord and a battery."

"You brought up a good point, but I don't want you doing anything with that phone. Stay inside the house. No matter what. Promise me?"

She folded her arms. "This is the worst. At least when we were on the run, we had distractions. Waiting around with no way to make contact, doing nothing is killing me."

Caleb's pocket vibrated. He pulled Jones's cell

from his pocket and glanced at the screen. "It's Jones."

Katherine's heart went into free fall with anticipation.

As soon as Caleb ended the call, he turned to her. "They found it. They found the proof. Leann had pictures linking Kane to murder. He must've had no idea she had evidence until recently."

"Doesn't do any good if they can't find Kane. Can't he live out the rest of his life in Mexico? With Noah? How will I ever get him back? I can't imagine leaving him to grow up with a monster like that." Panic thumped a fresh course of adrenaline through Katherine's veins. She didn't want to think about never seeing her nephew again.

"We don't know that. Jones has men in Dallas all over it."

His words were meant to be comforting. They weren't. A jagged rock ripped through her chest. Breathing hurt. She'd wait like a sitting duck for how long? Kane's men would never leave her alone. He wouldn't be satisfied until she was dead. "What about Scarface? Did he talk?"

"That's the best part. He did. Kane has been hiding in a warehouse downtown in the garment district. He's believed to be there right now. Jones is going after him. Coleman is on his way with reinforcements."

A myriad of emotions ran through her. Fear for

Noah gripped her. Could they get to him in time? A trill of hope rocketed. This whole ordeal could be behind them by morning's light.

A disturbance out front caught their attention.

"Wait here." Caleb moved to the cabinet and pulled out a handgun.

He crossed to her and placed it in her hand. Katherine's hand shook as she recoiled. "Not a good idea. I'm scared to death of those things."

"I won't leave you here without a way to protect yourself. It's a .38. You have to cock it to fire. Like this." He pressed her thumb to the hammer. "Then you point and pull the trigger. Wait here for me, but if someone comes through that door you don't recognize, shoot."

A lump in Katherine's throat made swallowing difficult. Her breathing came in spasms and her chest hurt. *Be strong. Refuse to be defeated.* She gripped the handle tighter. "Okay."

"I better check on Matt." Caleb kissed her forehead. He turned and headed toward the front of the house. "Don't be afraid to use the gun if you need to. Look before you shoot."

All her danger signals were flaring, and she knew on instinct something very bad was about to go down. They'd found her. Fear crippled her, freezing every muscle of her body even though she had the very real sense she was shaking on the outside. Sweat beaded and dripped down her forehead like the trickle of melting ice cream.

She couldn't let Caleb go alone.

Her eyes had already adjusted to the darkness, so finding her way around outside the house wasn't a problem. At the last corner, she crouched low, making herself as small as possible, and moved behind the Japanese boxwoods in the front land-scaping. Caleb stepped out the front door with his right arm extended, gun aimed.

Matt was on his knees in front of the house with his arms and legs bound. A man the size of a linebacker stood behind him, his gun pointed at his head.

Oh. God. No.

She turned away for an instant, unable to look. Guilt this was all her fault gripped her.

"He has nothing to do with this. Let him go." Caleb's voice was surprisingly even. He was calm under pressure whereas Katherine's nerves were fried.

The sound of gravel crunching underneath tires brought her focus to the road where a blacked-out SUV barreled down the path.

"Doesn't seem like your friend here wants to get up," said the linebacker, kicking Matt from behind.

Katherine prayed Caleb wouldn't react to the taunting.

A thousand ideas ran through her head. Should

she slip into the house and call 9-1-1? Wasn't Coleman on his way? She crouched low, rooted to her spot as two men stepped out of the SUV. One she recognized from Noah's kidnapping, the other was new. He was smaller than the others, but wore an expensive suit. His hair was dark, curly and slicked back. Kane?

"Put your gun down on the porch, and we'll consider sparing your life," the familiar one said.

Caleb didn't budge.

"Fine. Then your buddy here gets a bullet in the head." He lowered the barrel toward Matt.

Caleb put up both hands in the universal sign for surrender. "No need to do that." He lowered his gun to the porch and kicked it forward with the toe of his boot.

"Where is she?" the man with the slicked-back dark hair asked, his tone clipped; there was that telltale albeit subtle difference in the way he pronounced his vowels.

Katherine knew exactly who he was. Kane.

"I'm afraid it's just us guys here," Caleb responded.

"Don't insult me. I happen to know you were with her. She must be here somewhere." Kane glanced around. "Come out. Come out. Wherever you are."

Kane walked closer to Caleb, eyeing him up and

down. He turned to his henchmen and pointed to Matt. "Show them we're serious."

The crack of a bullet split the night air.

Katherine's heart plummeted. A gasp escaped before she could squash it. She fought the urge to vomit. Make a noise and Kane had what he wanted. *Her.* Game over.

She forced herself to peer through the bushes at him, expecting to see blood splattered on the men. There was none. If they hadn't shot Matt, what had they hit?

The bullet must've pinged the ground instead. Thank God. No one was hurt.

A wicked grin crossed Kane's attractive features. Authority and power radiated from him. Underneath that good-looking exterior, this man was the devil reincarnate. How horrible was he? Leann was a good person. How could she have gotten involved with such evil?

Katherine remembered the practiced, cool voice she'd first heard on the phone. Was that the one he'd used to lure Leann? If she'd seen the other side to him, no wonder she'd wanted to escape. She must've innocently believed she could keep him away from Noah. That definitely had to be why she'd moved around so much. It all made sense now. She'd kept the evidence quiet, waiting until the day he showed up again. And when he'd found her? She'd decided to play him while she'd gone to the Feds for help. A new life. A new identity. She and Noah would be hidden forever.

The cost?

She would have to cross the father of her child.

That couldn't have been easy. Sadness and anger burned Katherine's chest, firing heat through her veins. Why hadn't Leann confided in her?

She didn't want to bring you down with her, a little voice said.

Oh, sister.

Kane glanced around wildly. "Still not wanting to come out and play. Well let's see if this changes your mind." He opened the back door to the SUV and lifted a small figure into his arms.

Noah?

Katherine's heart faltered. She feared it would stop beating altogether if her nephew was dead. Kane was a horrible man. Would he hurt his own son?

No. A man who made sure the boy had his medicine wouldn't harm him.

But he would kill Matt. Possibly even Caleb.

She had to stop him.

Without thinking, she tucked the gun into the band of her shorts and stepped out of the boxwoods. There was no way she could hit him from this far. Not with the way her hands were shaking. If she could get close enough, she'd take that bastard out with one shot. His henchmen might retaliate, but at least Kane would die. "I'm right here, you son of a bitch. You don't have to hurt any more innocent people."

Caleb made a move toward her but backed off when Kane aimed his gun at Noah's temple.

"Don't be a hero, cowboy," Kane said, smooth and practiced. "I've been waiting for this day for a long time. You won't ruin it for me, will you? No one's going to wreck my plans. No one sends me to jail." He turned to face Katherine. "Not that bitch sister of yours. And sure as hell not you. She said she loved me. All the time she was sneaking around behind my back. Talking to the Feds. How could she love me when she stabbed me in the back? What about you? Will you betray him, too? Let's see how much you care about your cowboy." He nodded toward his henchman, who moved behind Caleb and pressed a gun to his back.

"Hurt him if you want. It won't bother me," Katherine lied.

She needed Kane to believe those words even though she could feel warmth traveling up her neck to her cheeks. She ignored it.

Convincing Kane she didn't love Caleb might be his only chance to live.

If she could distract Kane long enough to pull the gun, and then fire, she'd stop him from hurting anyone else. He wasn't more than five feet away. So close she could smell his musky aftershave.

Too far to make a move before Kane's guy had a chance to pull the trigger and end Caleb's life.

She couldn't get a clear shot while Kane held Noah anyway. Thank God he was sleeping. She had to get that monster away from her nephew and focused on her.

"Besides, he doesn't know anything. But I do. And I'll testify. You'll rot in jail with all the other scum who think they're above the law."

"Scum?" Kane's voice raised another octave. "That's what your sister said about me?" The pained look on his face said he still loved Leann.

"Don't believe her. I know exactly what you did. I can point authorities to the evidence, too, and she can't," Caleb said quickly.

Damn him. Didn't he see what she was trying to do? He was going to get himself killed.

"He's wrong. This is between you and me. Let Noah get out of here. Matt can take him. And I'll do anything you want." Noah blinked up at her. Fear filled his brown eyes. He couldn't possibly know how much she loved him. And if they saw how important Caleb was to her, he'd be dead, too.

"Let my son go? My son? Your sister tried to keep him from me. No one will ever keep me from my boy again." Kane's voice bordered on hysteria. The high-pitch sound echoed in the night. "Do something to the friend."

The linebacker hit Matt with the butt of his gun.

Matt crumpled forward. Didn't move again.

Was he unconscious? Alive? He had to be.

Tears welled in her eyes. She sniffed them back. She couldn't afford to let her emotions take control.

A bolt of lightning raced sideways across the sky. A clap of thunder followed moments later.

If she were going to stop Kane, she had to act fast.

Caleb spun around and disarmed the man on him. The pair tumbled onto the ground in a twist of arms and legs.

Katherine used the distraction to slip her hand behind her and grip the gun. She fired a shot and the linebacker went down. Before she could locate Kane, he was next to her, his hand gripping her neck, and it felt like her eyes might pop out.

Another shot rang out.

Chapter Seventeen

Katherine forced herself to look at Caleb, expecting her own exploding pain to register at any moment. Everything had happened so fast, her brain almost couldn't catalog the sequence. Both he and the man on him lay still. Blood. There was so much blood. *Please move, Caleb. Get up.*

He didn't.

Hopelessness engulfed her. If he was dead… Oh, God… She couldn't even think what she would do without him.

Tears sprang from her eyes. She doubled over. Her world imploded around her. She'd finally invested herself and fallen in love. Now he was dead. Just like her parents. Just like her sister.

Leann.

Noah was sick. Would he die, too?

A hand gripped her shoulder, pulling her upright. Cold metal poked her back. She jerked away, spun around and stared into the blackest set of eyes she'd ever seen. "You killed him. This is your fault. You caused me to drop my son, too. That won't be forgiven."

Through blurry eyes she searched for Noah. He'd been placed on a seat in the SUV. The door was open.

Her gaze flew to Matt's lifeless body.

"He's still alive. For the moment. Make another move and he'll be dead, too," Kane said into her ear, disarming her. "You're going to pay for what that bitch sister of yours tried to do to me. I loved her. I treated her like a queen. Look what she did." He waved his gun around, and then pressed the metal barrel against Katherine's temple. "I never would've known if she hadn't gone and gotten herself killed. I pieced it together when I was going through her things. Nobody betrays me and gets away with it."

She squeezed her eyes shut.

"Now move," he growled.

Every muscle in her body stiffened as she forced herself by sheer will to walk. He pushed her toward the barn. The man behind her directed her actions. This was something new to fear. A crazed psychopath who wanted to do more than kill her. He needed to see her suffer.

"You won't get away with this," she said in the dark. His icy fingers gripped her neck. Her body convulsed. She could feel his hot breath on her.

"I'm going send you to meet that bitch sister of

yours in death. But first, you're going to watch that boyfriend of yours burn."

Katherine's heart shriveled. The air thinned. She struggled to take a breath. She refused to believe Caleb was gone and her life would end like this. That Noah would be brought up by this monster. There had to be a way out.

He tossed her into a stall and on top of a bale of hay. She popped up. "The cops are coming. They'll arrest you. Hurting me won't help your case. It'll only make it worse. If you leave now, you can disappear. They won't find you if you stay out of the country."

"Be still, kitten." He knocked her down, forced her hands behind her back and tied them together. "I have no plans to rot in jail. Time to get rid of the evidence."

Her body shuddered at his touch. She kicked as hard as she could, connecting with his shin multiple times.

He flinched and slapped her across the left cheek. Katherine's head jolted. It felt as though her eye would explode. A fresh course of adrenaline pumped through her.

"You're about to learn something." A wicked grin spread across his lips. "Look at me."

He touched her cheek with the back of his hand. "She favored you. So beautiful." He shook his head. "She could have had anything she wanted. I would have given her the world."

His lips thinned. His gaze narrowed. "Now you all die." He shook his head. "What a waste."

Katherine struggled against her bindings. The rope cut through her flesh. She ignored the pain, trying to loosen the ties.

A hysterical laugh brought her focus back to Kane.

"Stay here, little one. I'll be right back."

Maybe Katherine could free herself before he returned. Her body convulsed. Yet she couldn't budge the ropes. Kicking did no good, either.

It felt as though Kane had been gone for eternity when he finally showed up, dragging a bloody lifeless body.

Her heart beat against her ribs in painful stabs. *Caleb.*

"One more to go and I'll finally be rid of you all," Kane said before he disappeared again.

Where was the sheriff? His men?

Katherine's gaze frantically searched for any sign of life in Caleb. She knew it was too much to hope he was still alive. Yet she had to be sure. She watched his chest for signs of movement. His broad chest rose and fell.

Or was she seeing what she wanted to?

Was he unconscious?

Katherine could've sworn she just saw Caleb surveying the area. Were his eyes open?

Yes. Definitely so. Her heart soared at the realization Caleb was alive. He brought a finger to his lips, the universal sign to keep quiet.

Matt was dragged in next. Katherine wanted to scream. She fought harder against the ropes.

Kane positioned Matt next to Caleb and threw a few fistfuls of hay on top of them. Her pulse beat in her throat. She was sure a red heat crawled up her neck. She put all her focus toward Caleb.

Kane hovered over Katherine. She kicked and threw her arms at him, trying to fight. He held out a match over the heap.

She looked toward the man she loved one more time. One wrong move and Kane would shoot. She needed to stall. To get his attention. She looked up at him. "Leann wouldn't want this. She never meant to hurt you. The Feds must've forced her to turn against you. I know she loved you."

Kane's laugh was haughty and arrogant. He trailed his finger along her jawline, and she saw Caleb's hands fist. Hope filled her chest.

"You are almost as beautiful as Leann," Kane said. "She was a free spirit. You, on the other hand, are a bit uptight. Even so, I could make you moan. The things I would like to do to you before I watch you burn…."

Allowing him to touch her and talk about her sister in that way nearly killed her.

He smoothed his hand across her red cheek. "I wish you hadn't made me do that to you."

Kane's dark eyes homed in on her. He brought a match to life with a flick of his nail and dropped it next to Caleb.

The moment Katherine moved, Caleb was on top of Kane. With a few quick jabs to the head, Kane's body slumped on top of her, pinning her to the ground. He was unconscious, but for how long?

A scream escaped before she could get her bearings and push him off. "I thought you were…"

"I'll be fine. I took a blow to the head. Scrambled a few things. Took a minute to shake. By the time I got my bearings again, I was being dragged to the barn."

She struggled against the ropes on her wrists, tears falling down her cheeks. When Caleb helped free her, they pulled Matt to his feet. He shook his head. Disoriented, he didn't seem able to hold his own weight.

"Help him outside." Caleb handed over Jones's cell. "Call 9-1-1. I have to put out the fire before it spreads."

Katherine dialed the emergency number as she bore some of Matt's heft, and walked outside the barn.

After giving her location and details to the operator, she helped Matt ease onto the ground.

A moment later, Caleb dashed to her side, a fire extinguisher in his hands. "It was contained. Didn't take much to put it out."

"The police are on their way." Katherine looked to Matt. "He's hurt, but conscious."

Max was at the door to the tack room. He stood sentinel, barking wildly.

Caleb's autumn-brown eyes pierced through her as he set the extinguisher down and told her to wait for him.

"No. I'm going with you," she insisted with a glance toward Matt.

He motioned for her to go.

Kane was moving toward the back of the tack room, trying to escape. He rounded on them.

Caleb shielded her with his body, pulling a gun from his waistband. Kane launched himself toward them. The gun fired as the two landed on the ground.

In a quick motion, Caleb straddled Kane. Blood was everywhere.

Panic momentarily stopped her heart. "Are you shot?"

He shook his head.

Kane gurgled blood before his gaze fixed and his expression turned vacant.

She dropped to her knees. Max ran to her. She cradled him. "It's over."

Caleb guided her to her feet where the little dog followed. "Let's get Noah."

His hand closed on hers as he led her outside.

Matt stood, still weak, and Caleb took some of his weight.

Another bolt of lightning cut across the sky as a droplet of rain fell.

An SUV was gone. Only the man who'd been shot remained, lifeless on the ground.

By the time they reached Noah, his face was pale. Katherine picked him up and hugged him. He let out a yelp.

Katherine embraced him tighter. "Oh, baby. You're safe."

His brown eyes were wide and tearful.

Caleb stood next to her. "Okay, little man. We're going to get you to the hospital."

Noah nodded. His bottom lip quivered as tears welled. He was too tired to cry. Not a good sign.

"Did the men bring your medicine, baby?"

He shook his head.

His breathing was shallow, and Katherine realized it was probably the reason he wasn't bawling. He didn't have the energy, which meant he needed medicine right away.

"You're safe," she repeated over and over again, hugging him tightly into her chest. He was fading, and she knew it. "Can you check the car for his medicine, Caleb?"

They searched the vehicle, pulling out the contents of the console and glove box, looking for the life-saving drugs.

Rain starting coming down in a steady rhythm as Katherine held on to her nephew, whispering quiet reassurances that he would be okay.

He *had* to be fine.

She glanced at Caleb and tensed at his worried expression. Noah's eyes rolled back in their sockets; he was losing his grip on consciousness.

"An ambulance is on its way. So is Coleman," Caleb said.

Katherine's tears mixed with rain, sending streaks down her face. "Come on, baby. Stay with me."

Her shoulders rocked as she released the tears she'd been holding far too long. They came out full force now. "When will that damn ambulance be here?"

She kissed Noah's forehead. His face was paler than before. His skin was cool and moist to the touch. Her heart thudded in her chest. "Caleb. Oh, God. Nothing can happen to him. Not now."

"The keys are still in the ignition." He hopped in the driver's side and motioned for her to climb in the passenger seat.

The SUV started on the first try. He glanced back at Matt. "Wait here for the sheriff?"

"Yes. Now go," Matt said.

Caleb glanced at his friend again.

"I'm fine. Get out of here."

The engine roared as Caleb gunned it.

Sirens and lights brought the first spark of hope.

Caleb flashed the headlamps as they cut off the ambulance at the top of the drive.

He hopped out of the driver's seat and crossed his arms over his head to signal they needed help. A paramedic scrambled out of the passenger seat as Katherine ran toward him with Noah in her arms. "Help him, please. He's not breathing. He has asthma and may not had medicine in a few days."

A paramedic took him from her arms and ran to the back of the ambulance as she followed. His hands worked quickly and efficiently.

"Has the patient been to the emergency room or used EMS in the past twenty-four to forty-eight hours?" he asked, not looking up.

"No. He was kidnapped. His skin was pale and his breathing shallow when I found him." A flood of tears spilled out of Katherine's eyes and into the rain.

Caleb's arm came around her, reassuring her. Protecting her.

The paramedic shot a sympathetic look toward her. "I'm going to administer a dose of epinephrine."

Another ambulance whirred past. *Matt.*

She turned to Caleb. "Go. Be with your friend. I have this covered. I know how worried you are about him."

Caleb's head shook emphatically. "I won't leave you to deal with this all by yourself."

There was that cowboy code again. "He's your best friend. And I need to know if he's going to be okay. I want you to check on him for both of us."

She could almost see the arguments clicking through his mind. How torn he had to be. "I'm serious. Go. I'm safe and Noah's getting the help he needs."

The paramedic started an IV and bagged him. "We've got to get the boy to the hospital. You can ride in the front," he said to Katherine before turning to Caleb. "You can follow behind in your vehicle."

"I'll go with Noah. You stay with Matt. I'll meet you at the hospital," Katherine said, determined. She was fine with Noah and he needed to make sure his friend was okay.

"I know that stubborn look. I'd rather stay with you but I won't argue," Caleb agreed, looking more than reluctant.

She gave him a quick kiss as he helped her into the passenger seat.

CALEB DROVE LIKE a bat out of hell down the drive. He parked the SUV and went to his friend.

Matt had an oxygen tube under his nose, and his forehead had been cleaned up from all the blood. His cut wasn't as bad as it had first looked.

Matt blinked up at Caleb. "What the hell are you doing here?"

"Checking on you."

Matt issued a grunt. "I'm not the one who needs you."

"Try telling her that," Caleb quipped.

Sheriff Coleman roared up and jogged toward them. "Sorry I'm late. I got called away to another county on an emergency. Got there and they said they never made the call."

"I'm sure you'll need a statement, but I have to get to the hospital and check on the little boy," Caleb said.

Coleman took Caleb's outstretched hand and shook it. "I can always drop by tomorrow if you'd like. Sounds like you guys have had one hell of a night already."

He nodded.

"I spoke to Dallas PD to make sure you were no longer a person of interest in their murder investigation," Coleman said with a tip of his hat. "You're fine. I'll get this mess cleaned up and be out of here before you return."

"Much obliged, Sheriff." The last thing Caleb wanted to do was to bring Katherine home to reminders of the horrors she and Noah had endured.

Coleman patted Caleb on the back. "You need a ride to the hospital?"

"No, thanks." He said goodbye and climbed into the cab of his pickup.

HE MADE IT to the hospital in record time and found Katherine sitting next to Noah's bed.

She looked up at him with those expressive eyes. "He's going to be fine. His skin is already pink and dry."

Relief flooded him as he pulled up a chair next to her. "Did they say when he'll be released?"

"Could be as early as tomorrow. They want to keep him overnight for observation."

"That's the best news I've heard today."

"It is."

He cupped her cheek. "Then why the sad face?"

"Nothing. How's Matt?"

"He'll be fine. They're bringing him in. Not that he likes the idea."

A knock at the door interrupted their conversation. Marshal Jones poked his head inside. "Katherine Harper?"

"Yes. That's me."

"Marshal," Caleb said, nodding.

Jones returned the acknowledgment.

"Could I have a word with Ms. Harper in the hallway?"

"As long as he can come with me." She moved to the door alongside Caleb who was already in motion.

"Not a problem," Jones said.

"Is everything all right, Marshal?" Her hand was moist from nerves.

Caleb gave it a reassuring squeeze.

"I didn't mean to worry you," Jones said. "I wanted to let you know what we found on the CD." He glanced from her to Caleb.

Katherine's hand came up to her chest. "What?"

"Turns out your sister videotaped Kane murdering a business associate. We've been watching him for years trying to gather evidence against him for other crimes. He was slick. Anytime we got close, witnesses disappeared."

Katherine's head bowed.

"Your sister outsmarted him. She went to great lengths to hide the evidence. She disappeared. Then he found her."

"I wonder why she didn't run straight to the police or you guys," Katherine said, wiping a tear from her eye.

Caleb pulled her close.

"She'd been on the run, trying to keep her son safe. She was young and scared," Jones said. "All she wanted was to give her son a life. When I finally made contact with her, she told me that if anything happened, she wanted Noah to be with you. Said you'd be the best mother he could possibly have."

Tears rolled down Katherine's cheeks.

"For what it's worth, I'm sorry. She was brave to do what she did," he said. "If not for the accident, she would've brought Kane to justice."

Katherine's gaze lifted, her chin came up. "Thanks. It means a lot to hear you say that."

He inclined his chin. "Emergency personnel tried to revive Kane at the scene. You should know he didn't survive. He'll never be able to hurt you or Noah again. We apprehended an SUV with his associates, and they'll be locked away for a long time."

"Thank you." Relief washed through her.

Jones excused himself as Caleb walked her back into Noah's room.

Katherine checked on her nephew before taking a seat next to Caleb on the sofa.

"You need anything? Coffee?" he asked.

"No. I want to be right here in case Noah wakes in this strange place." Her eyes were rimmed with tears when she said, "I'm sorry you couldn't stay with your friend."

"Are you kidding? He was pissed at me for leaving you."

Confusion knitted her eyebrows. "I didn't want you to have to choose between us and him. He's your best friend."

"And he always will be. Did you think you were doing me some kind of favor pushing me away like that?"

"Yes. Noah was fine, and I needed to know how Matt was doing."

"That so?"

"Yes." She looked at him as if he had three eyes. "Besides, you don't know what it's like to have a family thrust on you before you're ready."

"As a matter of fact, I do. And guess what? It doesn't scare me. You make a decision and then adjust your life to adapt to it. I'm a grown man." He pulled her into his arms and felt her melt into his chest. "And I want you."

Tears spilled from her eyes, dotting his T-shirt. "I want you, too," she admitted.

"Let's make a deal."

She arched an eyebrow. "I'm listening."

"Let me tell you what I can and can't handle when we go home."

"Okay." Her smile didn't reach her eyes.

"You gonna explain the long face?"

"You have the ranch. Where's *home* for me and Noah? We can't go back to my apartment. Not after what happened."

"I was getting to that. I want you both to come

to live with me. I love you. My life was empty until you came along. If you don't like the ranch, we'll buy a new place. I belong wherever you are."

"Are you serious?" She looked as though she needed a minute to let his words sink in. Her head shook. "You love that place."

"Not as much as I love you."

"I love you, too. Believe me. I do. But what about Noah? I'm the only family he's got and I don't want to confuse him."

"Then let's change that."

Her expression made him think the three eyes she'd seen on his forehead had grown wings. "All I'm saying is let's make it permanent. *Us.* I want to become a family."

She looked up at him wide-eyed as he stood.

He got down on one knee. "If I live another hundred years, I know in my heart I won't meet anyone else like you. You fit me in every possible way that matters. I don't want you to leave. Ever. I want to spend my life chasing away your fears and seeing every one of your smiles. I'm asking you to be my wife."

Tears fell from her eyes.

He leaned forward and thumbed one away as it stained her cheek, and he waited for her answer.

She kissed him. Deep. Passionate. And it stirred his desire. "Keep that up, and I'll show you what we can do with the bed on the other side of that curtain while little man sleeps."

She smiled up at him and his heart squeezed.

"You haven't answered my question."

"Yes, Caleb, I will marry you."

"Good, because I want to start working on a new project."

"A project?" she echoed, raising her brow.

He pulled her into his chest and crushed his lips against hers. "I want Noah to have a little brother or sister running around soon."

She smiled. "I want that, too."

"And I'm going to spend the rest of my life loving you."

* * * * *